Collector's Library

KING HENRY THE FIFTH

KING HENRY
THE FIFTH

William Shakespeare

Introduction by
Ned Halley

Collector's Library

This edition published in 2011 by
Collector's Library
an imprint of CRW Publishing Limited,
69 Gloucester Crescent, London NW1 7EG

ISBN 978 1 907360 11 4

2 4 6 8 10 9 7 5 3 1

Typeset in Great Britain by
Bookcraft Ltd, Stroud, Gloucestershire

Printed and bound in China by Imago

Contents

INTRODUCTION

Shakespeare liked history. More than one in three of his plays owe their storylines to the lives of real people, from the Roman upstart Coriolanus in the fifth century BC to Henry VIII, whose eventful reign ended just a few years before Shakespeare's birth. The Bard, who borrowed the plots, in whole or part, of all his plays from earlier sources, factual or fictional, knew historical dramas about British sovereigns went down particularly well with audiences. Today's popular obsession with royal affairs – their loves and marriages as well as their intrigues and wars – is the perpetuation of a very old custom indeed.

The Chorus that opens Act I (and every other act) of *Henry V*, grandly proclaims the play's vaunting intent to depict the magnificence of its central figure, the King, and his achievements:

> O for a Muse of fire, that would ascend
> The brightest heaven of invention,
> A kingdom for a stage, princes to act
> And monarchs to behold the swelling scene!

The address quickly moves on to apologizing for the playwright's impertinence in trying to convey the glories of the monarch in a mere theatre. He seeks pardon for the players that they should dare

> On this unworthy scaffold to bring forth
> So great an object: can this cockpit hold
> The vasty fields of France? or may we cram
> Within this wooden O the very casques
> That did affright the air at Agincourt?

This prologue fulfils the dual function of setting the exciting theme of the play and of reassuring the ruling class that the utmost loyalty to the Crown will be observed

vii

throughout. It's a wise precaution. In Shakespeare's own lifetime, his works were staged not just in London theatres such as the Curtain and the Globe, but in the principal royal palace of the city, Whitehall. Queen Elizabeth I and from 1603 her successor King James I almost certainly joined the courtly audiences gathered in the palace's Banqueting Hall for performances. There is no sure evidence that the Queen saw *Henry V* – it was written late in her reign, in 1599, when she was somewhat withdrawn from public life and in declining health – but she would have approved heartily of its theme. Henry V, who died in 1422, was remembered among the most glorious of medieval monarchs, a strong, unifying ruler at home and a courageous champion of England's interests abroad. He and the Virgin Queen had much in common.

The play makes plenty of reference to the connections. Much is made of King Henry's Welshness. He was a Plantagenet, but born at Monmouth. Elizabeth was the last Tudor, a Welsh dynasty founded by soldier Owen Tudor, who fought at Agincourt and later married Henry V's widow, Catherine of Valois. Their grandson became Henry VII, the first Tudor monarch, and grandfather of Elizabeth.

In the play, Henry V is embarking on war with France in pursuit of the rightful claim he says he has on the French throne. He is denied it under the Salic Law, which barred succession to the crown of France by, or through, women. Edward III, Henry's great grandfather, had claimed the throne of France through his mother Isabel, sister of French king Charles IV, after her brother's death in 1328, but the throne was seized by Philip VI, the first Valois king of France. In 1337, determined to press his claim, Edward III invaded France, igniting the conflict we now know as the Hundred Years War. While Edward won spectacular battles including Crecy in 1346 and Poitiers in 1356, securing Normandy, he did not succeed in taking over the French crown before his death in 1377. When his later successor Henry V invaded France in 1415, he was merely continuing the same conflict, with the same avowed aim.

Had Salic Law pertained in England, Elizabeth would not have become Queen. This might have encouraged Shakespeare, as a loyal subject, to pen the Archbishop of Canterbury's long disquisition on the matter in Act I Scene 2 of *Henry V*. The prelate tells the King the law was a thoroughly dubious piece of discrimination favoured in the ninth century by Charles the Great, better known now as Charlemagne, Christian conqueror of large parts of Europe and prototype Holy Roman Emperor. This zealous king of the Franks, says the Archbishop, subscribed to a convention laid down by the first of all Frankish kings, Pharamond (probably a mythical figure), who had ruled over the German lands between the rivers Elbe and Sala until he died back in 426, and held 'in disdain the German women/ For some dishonest manners of their life'. He had consequently imposed the 'Salique' law to ensure no female would succeed him, ever. French dynasties, says Canterbury, subsequently co-opted this irrelevant impost in their own illegitimate interests. The Archbishop finally rules Salic Law a heresy, quoting no less an authority than the Old Testament on the matter:

> For in the book of Numbers is it writ,
> When the man dies, let the inheritance
> Descend unto the daughter.

If it seems curious that the King should consult the clergy about his claim on the French throne, in effect seeking permission to wage war, it's worth knowing that at this time, the church was vastly rich and wielded power in state matters. Churchmen and statesmen were interchangeable. This of course is the Pre-Reformation Catholic Church, a very much more political entity than the Anglican church of Shakespeare's time. So significant is the role of the church that Shakespeare opens the play with a scene between two senior clerics scheming to encourage the King to go to war, partly because it might distract him from one of his policies at home, namely reform of the church. This, they fear, would extend to depriving it of much of its wealth (exactly what Henry VIII was to do 120 years later). Canterbury warns his colleague the Bishop of Ely (one of the richest of all England's sees) that the bill in parliament

> If it pass against us,
> We lose the better half of our possession:
> For all the temporal lands which men devout
> By testament have given to the church
> Would they strip from us

Henry V did have plans to dispossess the church, and had to contend with the powerful reform movement the Lollards, who believed in the word of the scriptures over the doctrine of the Catholic church, and were not immune from stirring up dangerous civil unrest. These were the last years of the Great Schism, in which the unity of the Roman church was torn apart when the French, then in political control of Rome, refused to accept the election of an Italian pope in 1378 and appointed their own French pontiff, based in Avignon. The nations of the western world divided over which pope to follow, and the church as a whole exposed itself to ridicule and doubt by claiming that two or even three direct descendants of St Peter, diametrically opposed to each other's views, could be representing the deity on Earth at the same time. It is among Henry V's less-recognised achievements that he steered the nation through this crisis, controlling the Lollard uprising as well as the turbulent church.

But Henry V is principally a play about the war. With his claim on the French throne unanimously backed by the church and his court, including his own brothers the dukes of Bedford and Gloucester, the King is ready to meet the ambassadors of the Dauphin of France. Note that it is the Dauphin, Louis, who is represented. History records that his father, King Charles VI, was insane at this time. Louis was de facto ruler but Shakespeare, who writes the king into the play, tactfully avoids mentioning this – perhaps because Charles VI was a direct ancestor of Queen Elizabeth.

In the masterly diplomatic conclusion to Act I Scene II, the tension is duly wound up as the Dauphin's envoy conveys his master's insults to the king by offering him a treasure chest as a peace token which turns out to contain nothing more than tennis balls. It is true that Henry V, then only about 28, was known as a keen sportsman, but he was a battle-hardened soldier too, and in response to this jest (which might well have some historical basis) he gives the ambassador a chilling warning:

> And tell the pleasant prince this mock of his
> Hath turn'd his balls to gun-stones; and his soul
> Shall stand sore charged for the wasteful vengeance
> That shall fly with them: for many a thousand widows
> Shall this his mock mock out of their dear husbands;
> Mock mothers from their sons, mock castles down;
> And some are yet ungotten and unborn
> That shall have cause to curse the Dauphin's scorn.

We are ready for war. Just as at the outset of Act I, the Chorus returns to set the scene, telling us 'Now all the youth of England are on fire' in anticipation of hostilities, but warning, too, of a fiendish French plot to assassinate the King as he embarks at Southampton. Three treacherous English noblemen have been bribed, we are told, to commit the deed. This crime was indeed planned in July 1415, but it was not inspired by the French. The chief conspirator, the Earl of Cambridge, was plotting the murder because he believed his brother-in-law Edmund Mortimer, a descendant of Edward III, had a better claim on the throne. Mortimer had heard of the plot from Cambridge and told King Henry, who had the participants promptly arrested and executed. The dramatic confrontation between the king and the conspirators at Southampton is drama pure and simple.

The opening scene of Act II, preceding the king's exciting set-to with the doomed plotters, is the first of the play's rather unexpected diversions into knockabout comedy. We are introduced, in a London street, to the soldiery who will embark with Henry for the French war, in the persons of Pistol, Nym and Bardolph. All are former servants of Sir John Falstaff, the comic companion of the dissolute Prince Hal, as Henry V then was, in the preceding *Henry IV* plays. But poor Sir John we discover, is dead (in spite of a promise in *Henry IV Part II* that Falstaff, hugely popular with Elizabethan audiences, would be back), and this perhaps serves to demonstrate that any connection between the Prince of the past and the King of the day is now at an end.

And so to France where we meet King Charles, his Dauphin and their commanders. The Dauphin is confident of victory, dismissing Henry as 'a vain, giddy, shallow, humorous youth,' but his father, portrayed entirely in possession of his wits, warns of the lessons of history:

> Witness our too much memorable shame
> When Cressy battle fatally was struck,
> And all our princes captiv'd by the hand
> Of that black name, Edward, Black Prince of Wales

The playwright has the benefit of hindsight. The tactical disaster that was to befall the French at Agincourt – an enormous army of willful, aristocratic, heavily armoured knights stuck in mud and picked off by arrows fired a great distance by a small corps of highly disciplined longbowmen – had been played out with very close symmetry seventy years previously, at Crecy.

The war proper begins with Act III at the walls of Harfleur, and King Henry's immortal address to his troops:

> Once more unto the breach, dear friends, once more;
> Or close the wall up with our English dead.
> In peace there's nothing so becomes a man
> As modest stillness and humility:
> But when the blast of war blows in our ears,
> Then imitate the action of the tiger;
> Stiffen the sinews, summon up the blood,
> Disguise fair nature with hard-favour'd rage

Here is Shakespeare at his stirring best, and here, too, he departs from the true history of events. In the play, Harfleur, then the main seaport of Normandy, rapidly surrenders. In truth, the siege lasted a month and cost the lives of thousands of English troops, many of them from the dysentery that broke out in the camps they made in the filthy marshes that surrounded the heavily fortified town. When Henry embarked in August, his army was perhaps a fifth of the size of the French force that awaited him, but by the time he reached Agincourt in October, the ratio was more like one to ten.

But he triumphed none the less. As many as 10,000 French were killed, including a large proportion of the nation's nobility. English dead numbered few more than a hundred. The great battle was indeed fought on St Crispin's Day, 25 October 1415. And Shakespeare very well imagined what Henry V would have said after the fighting subsided:

> We few, we happy few, we band of brothers;
> For he to-day that sheds his blood with me
> Shall be my brother; be he ne'er so vile,
> This day shall gentle his condition:
> And gentlemen in England now a-bed
> Shall think themselves accursed they were not here,
> And hold their manhoods cheap whiles any speaks
> That fought with us upon Saint Crispin's day.

They are among the most moving lines of poetry in the English language. To many of us living in the 21st century, they are familiar from the epic screen versions of the play made in 1944, with Laurence Olivier as the king, and in 1989 starring Kenneth Branagh, and it seems certain that for countless generations yet to come, the imagined words of a very real soldier and monarch of the Middle Ages will continue to resonate, in times of peace, and in time of war.

Henry did win his war, reaching Paris in 1419 and the following year signing a treaty with Charles VI which disinherited the Dauphin. Henry was named the heir and in 1420 married Catherine de Valois. He was also instrumental in reunifying the papacy and bringing an end to the Great Schism by engineering the election of Pope Martin V. Henry was in effect the military, economic, even spiritual, leader of Europe. He was revered at home in England, but when the Dauphin rose against him in France he returned there in 1421, not long after learning that his bride was pregnant with their first child. Laying siege to the city of Meaux the next year, Henry contracted dysentery and died. He was only 34, and had never seen his son.

PISTOL Bid him prepare, for I will cut his throat.

KING HENRY THE FIFTH

DRAMATIS PERSONAE

KING HENRY THE FIFTH.
DUKE OF GLOSTER, ⎫
DUKE OF BEDFORD, ⎬ *brothers to the King.*
DUKE OF EXETER, *uncle to the King.*
DUKE OF YORK, *cousin to the King.*
EARL OF SALISBURY.
EARL OF WESTMORELAND.
EARL OF WARWICK.
ARCHBISHOP OF CANTERBURY.
BISHOP OF ELY.
EARL OF CAMBRIDGE.
LORD SCROOP.
SIR THOMAS GREY.
SIR THOMAS ERPINGHAM, GOWER, FLUELLEN,
    MACMORRIS, JAMY, *officers in King Henry's army.*
JOHN BATES, ALEXANDER COURT, MICHAEL
    WILLIAMS, *soldiers in the same.*
PISTOL.
NYM.
BARDOLPH.
BOY.
A HERALD.
CHARLES THE SIXTH, *King of France.*
LOUIS, *the Dauphin.*
DUKE OF BURGUNDY.
DUKE OF ORLEANS.
DUKE OF BOURBON.
THE CONSTABLE OF FRANCE.
RAMBURES, GRANDPRÉ, *French lords.*
GOVERNOR OF HARFLEUR.
MONTJOY, *a French herald.*
AMBASSADORS *to the King of England.*

1

ISABEL, *Queen of France.*
KATHARINE, *daughter to Charles and Isabel.*
ALICE, *a lady attending on her.*
HOSTESS *of a tavern in Eastcheap (formerly Mistress Quickly, and now married to Pistol).*

LORDS, LADIES, OFFICERS, SOLDIERS, CITIZENS, MESSENGERS, *and* ATTENDANTS.

CHORUS.

SCENE — *England; afterwards France.*

PROLOGUE

Enter CHORUS.

CHORUS

O for a Muse of fire, that would ascend
The brightest heaven of invention, —
A kingdom for a stage, princes to act,
And monarchs to behold the swelling scene!
Then should the warlike Harry, like himself,
Assume the port of Mars; and at his heels,
Leash'd-in like hounds, should famine, sword, and fire,
Crouch for employment. But pardon, gentles all,
The flat unraised spirits that have dared
On this unworthy scaffold to bring forth
So great an object: can this cockpit hold
The vasty fields of France? or may we cram
Within this wooden O the very casques
That did affright the air at Agincourt?
O, pardon! since a crooked figure may
Attest in little place a million;
And let us, ciphers to this great accompt,
On your imaginary forces work.
Suppose within the girdle of these walls
Are now confin'd two mighty monarchies,
Whose high-upreared and abutting fronts
The perilous narrow ocean parts asunder:
Piece-out our imperfections with your thoughts;
Into a thousand parts divide one man,
And make imaginary puissance;
Think, when we talk of horses, that you see them
Printing their proud hoofs i'th' receiving earth; —
For 'tis your thoughts that now must deck our kings,
Carry them here and there; jumping o'er times,
Turning th'accomplishment of many years
Into an hour-glass: for the which supply,
Admit me Chorus to this history;
Who, prologue-like, your humble patience pray,
Gently to hear, kindly to judge, our play.   [*Exit.*

ACT I

SCENE I

London. An ante-chamber in the KING'S *palace.*

Enter the ARCHBISHOP OF CANTERBURY *and the* BISHOP OF ELY.

ARCHBISHOP OF CANTERBURY
My lord, I'll tell you, — that self bill is urged,
Which in th'eleventh year of the last king's reign
Was like, and had indeed against us pass'd,
But that the scambling and unquiet time
Did push it out of further question.

BISHOP OF ELY
But how, my lord, shall we resist it now?

ARCHBISHOP OF CANTERBURY
It must be thought on. If it pass against us,
We lose the better half of our possession;
For all the temporal lands, which men devout
By testament have given to the church,
Would they strip from us; being valued thus, —
As much as would maintain, to the king's honour,
Full fifteen earls and fifteen hundred knights,
Six thousand and two hundred good esquires;
And, to relief of lazars and weak age,
Of indigent faint souls past corporal toil,
A hundred almshouses right well supplied;
And to the coffers of the king, beside,
A thousand pounds by th'year: thus runs the bill.

BISHOP OF ELY
This would drink deep.

ARCHBISHOP OF CANTERBURY
     'Twould drink the cup and all.

BISHOP OF ELY
But what prevention?

4

ARCHBISHOP OF CANTERBURY

  The king is full of grace and fair regard.

BISHOP OF ELY

  And a true lover of the holy church.

ARCHBISHOP OF CANTERBURY

  The courses of his youth promis'd it not.
  The breath no sooner left his father's body,
  But that his wildness, mortified in him,
  Seem'd to die too; yea, at that very moment,
  Consideration, like an angel, came,
  And whipp'd th'offending Adam out of him,
  Leaving his body as a paradise,
  T'envelop and contain celestial spirits.
  Never was such a sudden scholar made;
  Never came reformation in a flood,
  With such a heady current, scouring faults;
  Nor never Hydra-headed wilfulness
  So soon did lose his seat, and all at once,
  As in this king.

BISHOP OF ELY

            We are blessed in the change.

ARCHBISHOP OF CANTERBURY

  Hear him but reason in divinity,
  And, all-admiring, with an inward wish
  You would desire the king were made a prelate:
  Hear him debate of commonwealth affairs,
  You would say it hath been all-in-all his study:
  List his discourse of war, and you shall hear
  A fearful battle render'd you in music:
  Turn him to any cause of policy,
  The Gordian knot of it he will unloose,
  Familiar as his garter: — that, when he speaks,
  The air, a charter'd libertine, is still,
  And the mute wonder lurketh in men's ears,
  To steal his sweet and honey'd sentences;
  So that the art and practic part of life
  Must be the mistress to this theoric:

Which is a wonder how his Grace should glean it,
Since his addiction was to courses vain;
His companies unletter'd, rude, and shallow;
His hours fill'd up with riots, banquets, sports;
And never noted in him any study,
Any retirement, any sequestration
From open haunts and popularity.

BISHOP OF ELY

The strawberry grows underneath the nettle,
And wholesome berries thrive and ripen best
Neighbour'd by fruit of baser quality:
And so the prince obscur'd his contemplation
Under the veil of wildness; which, no doubt,
Grew like the summer grass, fastest by night,
Unseen, yet crescive in his faculty.

ARCHBISHOP OF CANTERBURY

It must be so; for miracles are ceas'd;
And therefore we must needs admit the means
How things are perfected.

BISHOP OF ELY

               But, my good lord,
How now for mitigation of this bill
Urg'd by the commons? Doth his majesty
Incline to it, or no?

ARCHBISHOP OF CANTERBURY

               He seems indifferent;
Or, rather, swaying more upon our part
Than cherishing th'exhibiters against us:
For I have made an offer to his majesty, —
Upon our spiritual convocation,
And in regard of causes now in hand,
Which I have open'd to his Grace at large,
As touching France, — to give a greater sum
Than ever at one time the clergy yet
Did to his predecessors part withal.

BISHOP OF ELY

How did this offer seem receiv'd, my lord?

ARCHBISHOP OF CANTERBURY

With good acceptance of his majesty;
Save that there was not time enough to hear —
As, I perceiv'd, his Grace would fain have done —
The severals and unhidden passages
Of his true titles to some certain dukedoms,
And, generally, to the crown and seat of France,
Deriv'd from Edward, his great-grandfather.

BISHOP OF ELY

What was th'impediment that broke this off?

ARCHBISHOP OF CANTERBURY

The French ambassador upon that instant
Crav'd audience; — and the hour, I think, is come
To give him hearing: is it four o'clock?

BISHOP OF ELY

It is.

ARCHBISHOP OF CANTERBURY

Then go we in, to know his embassy;
Which I could, with a ready guess, declare,
Before the Frenchman speak a word of it.

BISHOP OF ELY

I'll wait upon you; and I long to hear it.   [*Exeunt.*

SCENE II

The same. The Presence-chamber.

Enter KING HENRY, GLOSTER, BEDFORD,
EXETER, WARWICK, WESTMORELAND, *and*
ATTENDANTS.

KING HENRY

Where is my gracious Lord of Canterbury?

EXETER

Not here in presence.

KING HENRY

                    Send for him, good uncle.

7

WESTMORELAND

Shall we call in th'ambassador, my liege?

KING HENRY

Not yet, my cousin: we would be resolved,
Before we hear him, of some things of weight,
That task our thoughts, concerning us and France.

Enter the ARCHBISHOP OF CANTERBURY *and the*
BISHOP OF ELY.

ARCHBISHOP OF CANTERBURY

God and his angels guard your sacred throne,
And make you long become it!

KING HENRY

       Sure, we thank you.
My learned lord, we pray you to proceed,
And justly and religiously unfold
Why the law Salique, that they have in France,
Or should, or should not, bar us in our claim:
And God forbid, my dear and faithful lord,
That you should fashion, wrest, or bow your reading,
Or nicely charge your understanding soul
With opening titles miscreate, whose right
Suits not in native colours with the truth;
For God doth know how many, now in health,
Shall drop their blood in approbation
Of what your reverence shall incite us to.
Therefore take heed how you impawn our person,
How you awake our sleeping sword of war:
We charge you, in the name of God, take heed;
For never two such kingdoms did contend
Without much fall of blood; whose guiltless drops
Are every one a woe, a sore complaint
'Gainst him whose wrongs give edge unto the swords
That make such waste in brief mortality.
Under this conjuration, speak, my lord;
For we will hear, note, and believe in heart
That what you speak is in your conscience wash'd
As pure as sin with baptism.

ARCHBISHOP OF CANTERBURY

    Then hear me, gracious sovereign, — and you peers,
    That owe yourselves, your lives, and services
    To this imperial throne. — There is no bar
    To make against your highness' claim to France
    But this, which they produce from Pharamond, —
    In terram Salicam mulieres ne succedant,
    'No woman shall succeed in Salique land':
    Which Salique land the French unjustly gloze
    To be the realm of France, and Pharamond
    The founder of this law and female bar.
    Yet their own authors faithfully affirm
    That the land Salique is in Germany,
    Between the floods of Sala and of Elbe;
    Where Charles the Great, having subdued the Saxons,
    There left behind and settled certain French;
    Who, holding in disdain the German women
    For some dishonest manners of their life,
    Establish'd then this law, — to wit, no female
    Should be inheritrix in Salique land:
    Which Salique, as I said, 'twixt Elbe and Sala,
    Is at this day in Germany call'd Meisen.
    Then doth it well appear, the Salique law
    Was not devised for the realm of France:
    Nor did the French possess the Salique land
    Until four hundred one and twenty years
    After defunction of King Pharamond,
    Idly suppos'd the founder of this law;
    Who died within the year of our redemption
    Four hundred twenty-six; and Charles the Great
    Subdued the Saxons, and did seat the French
    Beyond the river Sala, in the year
    Eight hundred five. Besides, their writers say,
    King Pepin, which deposed Childeric,
    Did, as heir general, being descended
    Of Blithild, which was daughter to King Clothair,
    Make claim and title to the crown of France.

Hugh Capet also, — who usurp'd the crown
Of Charles the Duke of Lorraine, sole heir male
Of the true line and stock of Charles the Great, —
To find his title with some shows of truth,
Though, in pure truth, it was corrupt and naught,
Convey'd himself as heir to th'Lady Lingare,
Daughter to Charlemain, who was the son
To Louis the emperor, and Louis the son
Of Charles the Great. Also King Louis the Tenth,
Who was sole heir to the usurper Capet,
Could not keep quiet in his conscience,
Wearing the crown of France, till satisfied
That fair Queen Isabel, his grandmother,
Was lineal of the Lady Ermengare,
Daughter to Charles the foresaid Duke of Lorraine:
By the which marriage the line of Charles the Great
Was re-united to the crown of France.
So that, as clear as is the summer's sun,
King Pepin's title, and Hugh Capet's claim,
King Louis his satisfaction, all appear
To hold in right and title of the female:
So do the kings of France unto this day;
Howbeit they would hold up this Salique law
To bar your highness claiming from the female;
And rather choose to hide them in a net
Than amply to imbar their crooked titles,
Usurp'd from you and your progenitors.

KING HENRY

May I with right and conscience make this claim?

ARCHBISHOP OF CANTERBURY

The sin upon my head, dread sovereign!
For in the Book of Numbers is it writ, —
When the man dies, let the inheritance
Descend unto the daughter. Gracious lord,
Stand for your own; unwind your bloody flag;
Look back into your mighty ancestors:
Go, my dread lord, to your great-grandsire's tomb,

From whom you claim; invoke his warlike spirit,
And your great-uncle's, Edward the Black Prince,
Who on the French ground play'd a tragedy,
Making defeat on the full power of France,
Whiles his most mighty father on a hill
Stood smiling to behold his lion's whelp
Forage in blood of French nobility.
O noble English, that could entertain
With half their forces the full pride of France,
And let another half stand laughing by,
All out of work and cold for action!

BISHOP OF ELY

Awake remembrance of these valiant dead,
And with your puissant arm renew their feats:
You are their heir; you sit upon their throne;
The blood and courage that renowned them
Runs in your veins; and my thrice-puissant liege
Is in the very May-morn of his youth,
Ripe for exploits and mighty enterprises.

EXETER

Your brother kings and monarchs of the earth
Do all expect that you should rouse yourself,
As did the former lions of your blood.

WESTMORELAND

They know your Grace hath cause and means and
  might;
So hath your highness; never king of England
Had nobles richer and more loyal subjects,
Whose hearts have left their bodies here in England,
And lie pavilion'd in the fields of France.

ARCHBISHOP OF CANTERBURY

O, let their bodies follow, my dear liege,
With blood and sword and fire to win your right:
In aid whereof we of the spirituality
Will raise your highness such a mighty sum
As never did the clergy at one time
Bring in to any of your ancestors.

KING HENRY

We must not only arm t'invade the French,
But lay down our proportions to defend
Against the Scot, who will make road upon us
With all advantages.

ARCHBISHOP OF CANTERBURY

They of those marches, gracious sovereign,
Shall be a wall sufficient to defend
Our inland from the pilfering borderers.

KING HENRY

We do not mean the coursing snatchers only,
But fear the main intendment of the Scot,
Who hath been still a giddy neighbour to us;
For you shall read that my great-grandfather
Never went with his forces into France,
But that the Scot on his unfurnish'd kingdom
Came pouring, like the tide into a breach,
With ample and brim fulness of his force;
Galling the gleaned land with hot assays,
Girding with grievous siege castles and towns;
That England, being empty of defence,
Hath shook and trembled at th'ill neighbourhood.

ARCHBISHOP OF CANTERBURY

She hath been then more fear'd than harm'd, my
liege;
For hear her but exampled by herself: —
When all her chivalry hath been in France,
And she a mourning widow of her nobles,
She hath herself not only well defended,
But taken, and impounded as a stray,
The King of Scots; whom she did send to France,
To fill King Edward's fame with prisoner kings,
And make her chronicle as rich with praise
As is the ooze and bottom of the sea
With sunken wrack and sumless treasuries.

WESTMORELAND

But there's a saying, very old and true, —

'If that you will France win,
            Then with Scotland first begin':
For once the eagle England being in prey,
To her unguarded nest the weasel Scot
Comes sneaking, and so sucks her princely eggs;
Playing the mouse in absence of the cat,
To spoil and havoc more than she can eat.

EXETER

It follows, then, the cat must stay at home:
Yet that is but a curs'd necessity,
Since we have locks to safeguard necessaries,
And pretty traps to catch the petty thieves.
While that the armed hand doth fight abroad,
Th'advised head defends itself at home;
For government, though high, and low, and lower,
Put into parts, doth keep in one concent,
Congreeing in a full and natural close,
Like music.

ARCHBISHOP OF CANTERBURY

            True: therefore doth heaven divide
The state of man in divers functions,
Setting endeavour in continual motion;
To which is fixed, as an aim or butt,
Obedience: for so work the honey-bees,
Creatures that, by a rule in nature, teach
The art of order to a peopled kingdom.
They have a king, and officers of sorts:
Where some, like magistrates, correct at home;
Others, like merchants, venture trade abroad;
Others, like soldiers, armed in their stings,
Make boot upon the summer's velvet buds;
Which pillage they with merry march bring home
To the tent-royal of their emperor:
Who, busied in his majesty, surveys
The singing masons building roofs of gold;
The civil citizens kneading-up the honey;
The poor mechanic porters crowding in
Their heavy burdens at his narrow gate;

The sad-eyed justice, with his surly hum,
Delivering o'er to executors pale
The lazy yawning drone. I this infer, —
That many things, having full reference
To one concent, may work contrariously:
As many arrows, loosed several ways,
Fly to one mark;
As many several ways meet in one town;
As many fresh streams meet in one self sea;
As many lines close in the dial's centre;
So may a thousand actions, once afoot,
End in one purpose, and be all well borne
Without defeat. Therefore to France, my liege.
Divide your happy England into four;
Whereof take you one quarter into France,
And you withal shall make all Gallia shake.
If we, with thrice such powers left at home,
Cannot defend our own doors from the dog,
Let us be worried, and our nation lose
The name of hardiness and policy.

KING HENRY

Call in the messengers sent from the Dauphin.
                    [Exeunt some ATTENDANTS.
Now are we well resolv'd; and, by God's help,
And yours, the noble sinews of our power,
France being ours, we'll bend it to our awe,
Or break it all to pieces: or there we'll sit,
Ruling in large and ample empery
O'er France and all her almost kingly dukedoms,
Or lay these bones in an unworthy urn,
Tombless, with no remembrance over them:
Either our history shall with full mouth
Speak freely of our acts, or else our grave,
Like Turkish mute, shall have a tongueless mouth,
Not worshipp'd with a waxen epitaph.
        Enter AMBASSADORS *of France, attended.*
Now are we well prepared to know the pleasure

Of our fair cousin Dauphin; for we hear
Your greeting is from him, not from the king.

FIRST AMBASSADOR

May't please your majesty to give us leave
Freely to render what we have in charge;
Or shall we sparingly show you far off
The Dauphin's meaning and our embassy?

KING HENRY

We are no tyrant, but a Christian king;
Unto whose grace our passion is as subject
As are our wretches fetter'd in our prisons:
Therefore with frank and with uncurbed
    plainness
Tell us the Dauphin's mind.

FIRST AMBASSADOR

                Thus, then, in few.
Your highness, lately sending into France,
Did claim some certain dukedoms, in the right
Of your great predecessor, King Edward the Third.
In answer of which claim, the prince our master
Says, that you savour too much of your youth;
And bids you be advis'd, there's naught in France
That can be with a nimble galliard won; —
You cannot revel into dukedoms there.
He therefore sends you, meeter for your spirit,
This tun of treasure; and, in lieu of this,
Desires you let the dukedoms that you claim
Hear no more of you. This the Dauphin speaks.

KING HENRY

What treasure, uncle?

EXETER

                Tennis-balls, my liege.

KING HENRY

We are glad the Dauphin is so pleasant with us;
His present and your pains we thank you for:
When we have match'd our rackets to these balls,
We will, in France, by God's grace, play a set

Shall strike his father's crown into the hazard.
Tell him he hath made a match with such a wrangler
That all the courts of France will be disturb'd
With chases. And we understand him well,
How he comes o'er us with our wilder days,
Not measuring what use we made of them.
We never valued this poor seat of England;
And therefore, living hence, did give ourself
To barbarous licence; as 'tis ever common
That men are merriest when they are from home.
But tell the Dauphin, I will keep my state,
Be like a king, and show my sail of greatness,
When I do rouse me in my throne of France:
For that I have laid by my majesty,
And plodded like a man for working-days;
But I will rise there with so full a glory,
That I will dazzle all the eyes of France,
Yea, strike the Dauphin blind to look on us.
And tell the pleasant prince, this mock of his
Hath turn'd his balls to gun-stones; and his soul
Shall stand sore charged for the wasteful vengeance
That shall fly with them: for many a thousand
    widows
Shall this his mock mock out of their dear husbands;
Mock mothers from their sons, mock castles down;
And some are yet ungotten and unborn
That shall have cause to curse the Dauphin's scorn.
But this lies all within the will of God,
To whom I do appeal; and in whose name,
Tell you the Dauphin, I am coming on,
To venge me as I may, and to put forth
My rightful hand in a well-hallow'd cause.
So, get you hence in peace; and tell the Dauphin,
His jest will savour but of shallow wit,
When thousands weep, more than did laugh at it. —
Convey them with safe conduct. — Fare you well.
                              [*Exeunt* AMBASSADORS.

16

KING HENRY Tell the Dauphin, his jest will savour but of shallow wit,
when thousands weep.

EXETER
  This was a merry message.

KING HENRY
  We hope to make the sender blush at it.
  Therefore, my lords, omit no happy hour
  That may give furtherance to our expedition;
  For we have now no thought in us but France,
  Save those to God, that run before our business.
  Therefore let our proportions for these wars
  Be soon collected, and all things thought upon

That may with reasonable swiftness add
More feathers to our wings; for, God before,
We'll chide this Dauphin at his father's door.
Therefore let every man now task his thought,
That this fair action may on foot be brought.

[Flourish. Exeunt.

ACT II

PROLOGUE

Enter CHORUS.

CHORUS

Now all the youth of England are on fire,
And silken dalliance in the wardrobe lies:
Now thrive the armourers, and honour's thought
Reigns solely in the breast of every man:
They sell the pasture now to buy the horse;
Following the mirror of all Christian kings,
With winged heels, as English Mercuries.
For now sits Expectation in the air,
And hides a sword from hilts unto the point
With crowns imperial, crowns, and coronets,
Promis'd to Harry and his followers.
The French, advis'd by good intelligence
Of this most dreadful preparation,
Shake in their fear; and with pale policy
Seek to divert the English purposes.
O England! — model to thy inward greatness,
Like little body with a mighty heart, —
What mightst thou do, that honour would thee do,
Were all thy children kind and natural!
But see thy fault! France hath in thee found out
A nest of hollow bosoms, which he fills
With treacherous crowns; and three corrupted men, —
One, Richard Earl of Cambridge; and the second,

Henry Lord Scroop of Masham; and the third,
Sir Thomas Grey, knight, of Northumberland, —
Have, for the gilt of France — O guilt indeed! —
Confirm'd conspiracy with fearful France;
And by their hands this grace of kings must die,
If hell and treason hold their promises,
Ere he take ship for France, and in Southampton.
Linger your patience on; and we'll digest
Th'abuse of distance; force a play.
The sum is paid; the traitors are agreed;
The king is set from London; and the scene
Is now transported, gentles, to Southampton, —
There is the playhouse now, there must you sit:
And thence to France shall we convey you safe,
And bring you back, charming the narrow seas
To give you gentle pass; for, if we may,
We'll not offend one stomach with our play.
But, till the king come forth, and not till then,
Unto Southampton do we shift our scene.

[*Exit.*

SCENE I

London. Before the Boar's-Head Tavern, Eastcheap.
Enter CORPORAL NYM *and* LIEUTENANT
BARDOLPH.

BARDOLPH

Well met, Corporal Nym.

NYM

Good morrow, Lieutenant Bardolph.

BARDOLPH

What, are Ancient Pistol and you friends yet?

NYM

For my part, I care not: I say little; but when time shall
serve, there shall be smites; — but that shall be as it
may. I dare not fight; but I will wink, and hold out mine

iron: it is a simple one; but what though? it will toast
cheese, and it will endure cold as another man's sword
will: and there's the humour of it.

BARDOLPH

I will bestow a breakfast to make you friends; and we'll
be all three sworn brothers to France: let's it be so, good
Corporal Nym.

NYM

Faith, I will live so long as I may, that's the certain of it;
and when I cannot live any longer, I will do as I may:
that is my rest, that is the rendezvous of it.

BARDOLPH

It is certain, corporal, that he is married to Nell Quickly:
and, certainly, she did you wrong; for you were troth-
plight to her.

NYM

I cannot tell: — things must be as they may: men may
sleep, and they may have their throats about them at
that time; and, some say, knives have edges. It must be
as it may: though patience be a tired mare, yet she will
plod. There must be conclusions. Well, I cannot tell.

BARDOLPH

Here comes Ancient Pistol and his wife: — good
corporal, be patient here.

Enter PISTOL *and* HOSTESS.

How now, mine host Pistol!

PISTOL

Base tike, call'st thou me host?
Now, by this hand, I swear, I scorn the term;
Nor shall my Nell keep lodgers.

HOSTESS

No, by my troth, not long; for we cannot lodge and board
a dozen or fourteen gentlewomen that live honestly by the
prick of their needles, but it will be thought we keep a
bawdy-house straight. [NYM *and* PISTOL *draw*.] O
well-a-day, Lady, if he be not drawn now! We shall see
wilful adultery and murder committed.

20

BARDOLPH

Good lieutenant, — good corporal, — offer nothing here.

NYM

Pish!

PISTOL

Pish for thee, Iceland dog! thou prick-ear'd cur of Iceland!

HOSTESS

Good Corporal Nym, show thy valour, and put up your sword.

NYM

Will you shog off? I would have you *solus*.

PISTOL

Solus, egregious dog? O viper vile!
The *solus* in thy most mervailous face;
The *solus* in thy teeth, and in thy throat,
And in thy hateful lungs, yea, in thy maw, perdy,
And, which is worse, within thy nasty mouth!
I do retort the *solus* in thy bowels;
For I can take, and Pistol's cock is up,
And flashing fire will follow.

NYM

I am not Barbason; you cannot conjure me. I have an humour to knock you indifferently well. If you grow foul with me, Pistol, I will scour you with my rapier, as I may, in fair terms: if you would walk off, I would prick your guts a little, in good terms, as I may: and that's the humour of it.

PISTOL

O braggart vile, and damned furious wight!
The grave doth gape, and doting death is near;
Therefore exhale.

BARDOLPH

Hear me, hear me what I say: — he that strikes the first stroke, I'll run him up to the hilts, as I am a soldier.

[*Draws.*

PISTOL

An oath of mickle might; and fury shall abate. —
Give me thy fist, thy fore-foot to me give:
Thy spirits are most tall. *[They sheath their swords.*

NYM

I will cut thy throat, one time or other, in fair terms: that
is the humour of it.

PISTOL

Couple a gorge!
That is the word. I thee defy again.
O hound of Crete, think'st thou my spouse to get?
No; to the spital go,
And from the powdering-tub of infamy
Fetch forth the lazar kite of Cressid's kind,
Doll Tearsheet she by name, and her espouse:
I have, and I will hold, the *quondam* Quickly
For the only she; and — *pauca*, there's enough.
Go to.

Enter BOY.

BOY

Mine host Pistol, you must come to my master, — and
you, hostess: — he is very sick, and would to bed. —
Good Bardolph, put thy face between his sheets, and do
the office of a warming-pan. — Faith, he's very ill.

BARDOLPH

Away, you rogue!

HOSTESS

By my troth, he'll yield the crow a pudding one of these
days: the king has kill'd his heart. — Good husband,
come home presently.

[Exeunt HOSTESS *and* BOY.

BARDOLPH

Come, shall I make you two friends? We must to France
together: why the devil should we keep knives to cut one
another's throats?

22

PISTOL

Let floods o'erswell, and fiends for food howl on!

NYM

You'll pay me the eight shillings I won of you at betting?

PISTOL

Base is the slave that pays.

NYM

That now I will have: that's the humour of it.

PISTOL

As manhood shall compound: push home.   [*They draw.*

BARDOLPH

By this sword, he that makes the first thrust, I'll kill him;
by this sword, I will.   [*Draws.*

PISTOL

Sword is an oath, and oaths must have their course.

BARDOLPH

Corporal Nym, an thou wilt be friends, be friends: an
thou wilt not, why, then, be enemies with me too.
Prithee, put up.

NYM

I shall have my eight shillings I won of you at betting?

PISTOL

A noble shalt thou have, and present pay;
And liquor likewise will I give to thee,
And friendship shall combine and brotherhood;
I'll live by Nym, and Nym shall live by me; —
Is not this just? — for I shall sutler be
Unto the camp, and profits will accrue.
Give me thy hand.   [*They sheathe their swords.*

NYM

I shall have my noble?

PISTOL

In cash most justly paid.

NYM

Well, then, that's the humour of it.

Enter HOSTESS.

HOSTESS

As ever you came of women, come in quickly to Sir
John. Ah, poor heart! he is so shaked of a burning
quotidian tertian, that it is most lamentable to behold.
Sweet men, come to him.

NYM

The king hath run bad humours on the knight, that's the
even of it.

PISTOL

Nym, thou hast spoke the right;
His heart is fracted and corroborate.

NYM

The king is a good king: but it must be as it may; he
passes some humours and careers.

PISTOL

Let us condole the knight; for, lambkins, we will live.

[*Exeunt.*

SCENE II

Southampton. A council-chamber.

Enter EXETER, BEDFORD, *and* WESTMORELAND.

BEDFORD

'Fore God, his Grace is bold, to trust these traitors.

EXETER

They shall be apprehended by and by.

WESTMORELAND

How smooth and even they do bear themselves!
As if allegiance in their bosoms sat,
Crowned with faith and constant loyalty.

BEDFORD

The king hath note of all that they intend,
By interception which they dream not of.

EXETER

Nay, but the man that was his bedfellow,
Whom he hath dull'd and cloy'd with gracious favours,

That he should, for a foreign purse, so sell
His sovereign's life to death and treachery!
Trumpets sound. Enter KING HENRY, CAMBRIDGE,
SCROOP, GREY, LORDS, *and* ATTENDANTS.

KING HENRY

Now sits the wind fair, and we will aboard.
My Lord of Cambridge, — and my kind Lord of
    Masham, —
And you, my gentle knight, — give me your thoughts:
Think you not that the powers we bear with us
Will cut their passage through the force of France,
Doing the execution and the act
For which we have in head assembled them?

SCROOP

No doubt, my liege, if each man do his best.

KING HENRY

I doubt not that; since we are well persuaded
We carry not a heart with us from hence
That grows not in a fair consent with ours,
Nor leave not one behind that doth not wish
Success and conquest to attend on us.

CAMBRIDGE

Never was monarch better fear'd and lov'd
Than is your majesty: there's not, I think, a subject,
That sits in heart-grief and uneasiness
Under the sweet shade of your government.

GREY

True: those that were your father's enemies
Have steep'd their galls in honey, and do serve you
With hearts create of duty and of zeal.

KING HENRY

We therefore have great cause of thankfulness;
And shall forget the office of our hand,
Sooner than quittance of desert and merit
According to the weight and worthiness.

SCROOP

So service shall with steeled sinews toil,

And labour shall refresh itself with hope,
To do your Grace incessant services.

KING HENRY

We judge no less. — uncle of Exeter,
Enlarge the man committed yesterday,
That rail'd against our person: we consider
It was excess of wine that set him on;
And, on his more advice, we pardon him.

SCROOP

That's mercy, but too much security:
Let him be punish'd, sovereign; lest example
Breed, by his sufferance, more of such a kind.

KING HENRY

O, let us yet be merciful.

CAMBRIDGE

So may your highness, and yet punish too.

GREY

Sir, you show great mercy, if you give him life,
After the taste of much correction.

KING HENRY

Alas, your too much love and care of me
Are heavy orisons 'gainst this poor wretch!
If little faults, proceeding on distemper,
Shall not be wink'd at, how shall we stretch our eye
When capital crimes, chew'd, swallow'd, and digested,
Appear before us? — We'll yet enlarge that man,
Though Cambridge, Scroop, and Grey, in their dear
    care
And tender preservation of our person,
Would have him punish'd. And now to our French
causes:
Who are the late commissioners?

CAMBRIDGE

I one, my lord:
Your highness bade me ask for it to-day.

SCROOP

So did you me, my liege.

26

GREY

And me, my royal sovereign.

KING HENRY

Then, Richard Earl of Cambridge, there is yours; —
There yours, Lord Scroop of Masham; — and, sir
    knight,
Grey of Northumberland, this same is yours: —
Read them; and know, I know your worthiness. —
My Lord of Westmoreland, and uncle Exeter,
We will aboard to-night. — Why, how now, gentlemen!
What see you in those papers, that you lose
So much complexion? — Look ye, how they change!
Their cheeks are paper. — Why, what read you there,
That hath so cowarded and chas'd your blood
Out of appearance?

CAMBRIDGE

            I do confess my fault;
And do submit me to your highness' mercy.

GREY and SCROOP

To which we all appeal.

KING HENRY

The mercy that was quick in us but late,
By your own counsel is suppress'd and kill'd:
You must not dare, for shame, to talk of mercy;
For your own reasons turn into your bosoms,
As dogs upon their masters, worrying you. —
See you, my princes and my noble peers,
These English monsters! My Lord of Cambridge
    here, —
You know how apt our love was to accord
To furnish him with all appertinents
Belonging to his honour; and this man
Hath, for a few light crowns, lightly conspired,
And sworn unto the practices of France,
To kill us here in Hampton: to the which
This knight, no less for bounty bound to us
Than Cambridge is, hath likewise sworn. — But, O,

What shall I say to thee, Lord Scroop? thou cruel,
Ingrateful, savage, and inhuman creature!
Thou that didst bear the key of all my counsels,
That knew'st the very bottom of my soul,
That almost mightst have coin'd me into gold,
Wouldst thou have practis'd on me for thy use, —
May it be possible, that foreign hire
Could out of thee extract one spark of evil
That might annoy my finger? 'tis so strange,
That, though the truth of it stands off as gross
As black and white, my eye will scarcely see it.
Treason and murder ever kept together,
As two yoke-devils sworn to either's purpose,
Working so grossly in a natural cause,
That admiration did not whoop at them:
But thou, 'gainst all proportion, didst bring in
Wonder to wait on treason and on murder:
And whatsoever cunning fiend it was
That wrought upon thee so preposterously,
Hath got the voice in hell for excellence:
All other devils, that suggest by treasons,
Do botch and bungle up damnation
With patches, colours, and with forms being fetch'd
From glistering semblances of piety;
But he that temper'd thee bade thee stand up,
Gave thee no instance why thou shouldst do treason,
Unless to dub thee with the name of traitor.
If that same demon that hath gull'd thee thus
Should with his lion-gait walk the whole world,
He might return to vasty Tartar back,
And tell the legions, 'I can never win
A soul so easy as that Englishman's.'
O, how hast thou with jealousy infected
The sweetness of affiance! Show men dutiful?
Why, so didst thou: seem they grave and learned?
Why, so didst thou: come they of noble family?
Why, so didst thou: seem they religious?

Why, so didst thou: or are they spare in diet;
Free from gross passion, or of mirth or anger;
Constant in spirit, not swerving with the blood;
Garnish'd and deck'd in modest complement;
Not working with the eye without the ear,
And but in purged judgement trusting neither?
Such and so finely bolted didst thou seem:
And thus thy fall hath left a kind of blot,
To mark the full-fraught man and best indued
With some suspicion. I will weep for thee;
For this revolt of thine, methinks, is like
Another fall of man. — Their faults are open:
Arrest them to the answer of the law; —
And God acquit them of their practices!

EXETER

I arrest thee of high treason, by the name of Richard
    Earl of Cambridge.
I arrest thee of high treason, by the name of
    Henry Lord Scroop of Masham.
I arrest thee of high treason, by the name of
    Thomas Grey, knight, of Northumberland.

SCROOP

Our purposes God justly hath discover'd;
And I repent my fault more than my death;
Which I beseech your highness to forgive,
Although my body pay the price of it.

CAMBRIDGE

For me, — the gold of France did not seduce;
Although I did admit it as a motive
The sooner to effect what I intended:
But God be thanked for prevention;
Which I in sufferance heartily will rejoice,
Beseeching God and you to pardon me.

GREY

Never did faithful subject more rejoice
At the discovery of most dangerous treason
Than I do at this hour joy o'er myself,

Prevented from a damned enterprise:
My fault, but not my body, pardon, sovereign.

KING HENRY

God quit you in his mercy! Hear your sentence.
You have conspired against our royal person,
Join'd with an enemy proclaim'd, and from his coffers
Receiv'd the golden earnest of our death;
Wherein you would have sold your king to slaughter,
His princes and his peers to servitude,
His subjects to oppression and contempt,
And his whole kingdom into desolation.
Touching our person, seek we no revenge;
But we our kingdom's safety must so tender,
Whose ruin you have sought, that to her laws
We do deliver you. Get you, therefore, hence,
Poor miserable wretches, to your death:
The taste whereof, God of his mercy give
You patience to endure, and true repentance
Of all your dear offences! — Bear them hence.
[*Exeunt* CAMBRIDGE, SCROOP, *and* GREY, *guarded.*
Now, lords, for France; the enterprise whereof
Shall be to you as us like glorious.
We doubt not of a fair and lucky war,
Since God so graciously hath brought to light
This dangerous treason, lurking in our way
To hinder our beginnings; we doubt not now
But every rub is smoothed on our way.
Then, forth, dear countrymen: let us deliver
Our puissance into the hand of God,
Putting it straight in expedition.
Cheerly to sea; the signs of war advance:
No king of England, if not king of France.   [*Exeunt.*

SCENE III

London. Before the Boar's-Head Tavern, Eastcheap.

Enter PISTOL, HOSTESS, NYM, BARDOLPH, *and*
BOY.

HOSTESS

Prithee, honey-sweet husband, let me bring thee to
Staines.

PISTOL

No; for my manly heart doth yearn. —
Bardolph, be blithe; — Nym, rouse thy vaunting veins; —
Boy, bristle thy courage up; — for Falstaff he is dead,
And we must yearn therefore.

BARDOLPH

Would I were with him, wheresome'er he is, either in
heaven or in hell!

HOSTESS

Nay, sure, he's not in hell: he's in Arthur's bosom, if
ever man went to Arthur's bosom. A' made a finer end,
and went away, an it had been any christom child; a'
parted ev'n just between twelve and one, ev'n at the
turning o'th'tide: for after I saw him fumble with the
sheets, and play with flowers, and smile upon his
fingers' ends, I knew there was but one way; for his nose
was as sharp as a pen, and a' babbled of green fields.
'How now, sir John!' quoth I: 'what, man! be o' good
cheer.' So a' cried out 'God, God, God!' three or four
times. Now I, to comfort him, bid him a' should not
think of God; I hoped there was no need to trouble
himself with any such thoughts yet. So a' bade me lay
more clothes on his feet: I put my hand into the bed and
felt them, and they were as cold as any stone; then I felt
to his knees, and they were as cold as any stone, and so
upward and upward, and all was as cold as any stone.

NYM

They say he cried out of sack.

HOSTESS

Ay, that a' did.

BARDOLPH

And of women.

HOSTESS

Nay, that a' did not.

BOY

Yes, that a' did; and said they were devils incarnate.

HOSTESS

A' could never abide carnation; 'twas a colour he
never liked.

BOY

A' said once, the devil would have him about women.

HOSTESS

A' did in some sort, indeed, handle women; but then he
was rheumatic, and talk'd of the whore of Babylon.

BOY

Do you not remember, a' saw a flea stick upon
Bardolph's nose, and a' said it was a black soul burning
in hell-fire?

BARDOLPH

Well, the fuel is gone that maintain'd that fire: that's all
the riches I got in his service.

NYM

Shall we shog? the king will be gone from Southampton.

PISTOL

Come, let's away. — My love, give me thy lips.
Look to my chattels and my movables:
Let senses rule; the word is 'Pitch and Pay';
Trust none;
For oaths are straws, men's faiths are wafer-cakes,
And hold-fast is the only dog, my duck:
Therefore, *caveto* be thy counsellor.
Go, clear thy crystals. — Yoke-fellows in arms,
Let us to France; like horse-leeches, my boys,
To suck, to suck, the very blood to suck!

BOY

And that's but unwholesome food, they say.

PISTOL

Touch her soft mouth, and march.

BARDOLPH

Farewell, hostess.   *[Kissing her.*

NYM

I cannot kiss, that is the humour of it; but, adieu.

PISTOL

Let housewifery appear: keep close, I thee command.

HOSTESS

Farewell; adieu.   *[Exeunt.*

SCENE IV

France. A room in the French KING'S *palace.*

Flourish. Enter the FRENCH KING, *the* DAUPHIN, *the*
DUKE OF BURGUNDY, *the* CONSTABLE, *and others*

FRENCH KING

Thus comes the English with full power upon us;
And more than carefully it us concerns
To answer royally in our defences.
Therefore the Dukes of Berri and of Bretagne,
Of Brabant and of Orleans, shall make forth, —
And you, Prince Dauphin, — with all swift dispatch,
To line and new repair our towns of war
With men of courage and with means defendant;
For England his approaches makes as fierce
As waters to the sucking of a gulf.
It fits us, then, to be as provident
As fear may teach us, out of late examples
Left by the fatal and neglected English
Upon our fields.

DAUPHIN

             My most redoubted father,
It is most meet we arm us 'gainst the foe;
For peace itself should not so dull a kingdom,
Though war nor no known quarrel were in question,
But that defences, musters, preparations,
Should be maintain'd, assembled, and collected,

As were a war in expectation.
Therefore, I say 'tis meet we all go forth
To view the sick and feeble parts of France:
And let us do it with no show of fear;
No, with no more than if we heard that England
Were busied with a Whitsun morris-dance:
For, my good liege, she is so idly king'd,
Her sceptre so fantastically borne
By a vain, giddy, shallow, humorous youth,
That fear attends her not.

CONSTABLE

                O peace, Prince Dauphin!
You are too much mistaken in this king:
Question your Grace the late ambassadors, —
With what great state he heard their embassy,
How well supplied with noble counsellors,
How modest in exception, and withal
How terrible in constant resolution, —
And you shall find his vanities forespent
Were but the outside of the Roman Brutus,
Covering discretion with a coat of folly;
As gardeners do with ordure hide those roots
That shall first spring and be most delicate.

DAUPHIN

Well, 'tis not so, my lord high-constable;
But though we think it so, it is no matter:
In cases of defence 'tis best to weigh
The enemy more mighty than he seems:
So the proportions of defence are fill'd;
Which, of a weak and niggardly projection,
Doth, like a miser, spoil his coat with scanting
A little cloth.

FRENCH KING

                Think we King Harry strong;
And princes, look you strongly arm to meet him.
The kindred of him hath been flesh'd upon us;
And he is bred out of that bloody strain

That haunted us in our familiar paths:
Witness our too-much memorable shame
When Cressy battle fatally was struck,
And all our princes captiv'd by the hand
Of that black name, Edward, Black Prince of Wales;
Whiles that his mountain sire, — on mountain standing,
Up in the air, crown'd with the golden sun, —
Saw his heroical seed, and smil'd to see him,
Mangle the work of nature, and deface
The patterns that by God and by French fathers
Had twenty years been made. This is a stem
Of that victorious stock; and let us fear
The native mightiness and fate of him.

Enter a MESSENGER.

MESSENGER
Ambassadors from Harry king of England
Do crave admittance to your majesty.

FRENCH KING
We'll give them present audience. Go, and bring them.
[*Exeunt* MESSENGER *and certain* LORDS.
You see this chase is hotly follow'd, friends.

DAUPHIN
Turn head, and stop pursuit; for coward dogs
Most spend their mouths, when what they seem to
    threaten
Runs far before them. Good my sovereign,
Take up the English short; and let them know
Of what a monarchy you are the head:
Self-love, my liege, is not so vile a sin
As self-neglecting.

Enter LORDS, *with* EXETER *and* TRAIN.

FRENCH KING
                        From our brother England?

EXETER
From him; and thus he greets your majesty.
He wills you, in the name of God Almighty,
That you divest yourself, and lay apart

35

The borrow'd glories, that, by gift of heaven,
By law of nature and of nations, 'longs
To him and to his heirs; namely, the crown,
And all wide-stretched honours that pertain,
By custom and the ordinance of times,
Unto the crown of France. That you may know
'Tis no sinister nor no awkward claim,
Pick'd from the worm-holes of long-vanish'd days,
Nor from the dust of old oblivion rak'd,
He sends you this most memorable line,   [*Gives a paper.*
In every branch truly demonstrative;
Willing to overlook this pedigree:
And when you find him evenly derived
From his most fam'd of famous ancestors,
Edward the Third, he bids you then resign
Your crown and kingdom, indirectly held
From him the native and true challenger.

FRENCH KING

Or else what follows?

EXETER

Bloody constraint; for if you hide the crown
Even in your hearts, there will he rake for it:
Therefore in fierce tempest is he coming,
In thunder and in earthquake, like a Jove,
That, if requiring fail, he will compel;
And bids you, in the bowels of the Lord,
Deliver up the crown; and to take mercy
On the poor souls for whom this hungry war
Opens his vasty jaws: and on your head
Turns he the widows' tears, the orphans' cries,
The dead men's blood, the pining maidens' groans,
For husbands, fathers, and betrothed lovers,
That shall be swallow'd in this controversy.
This is his claim, his threatening, and my message;
Unless the Dauphin be in presence here,
To whom expressly I bring greeting too.

FRENCH KING

For us, we will consider of this further:
To-morrow shall you bear our full intent
Back to our brother England.

DAUPHIN

                      For the Dauphin,
I stand here for him: what to him from England?

EXETER

Scorn and defiance; slight regard, contempt,
And any thing that may not misbecome
The mighty sender, doth he prize you at.
Thus says my king: an if your father's highness
Do not, in grant of all demands at large,
Sweeten the bitter mock you sent his majesty,
He'll call you to so hot an answer of it,
That caves and womby vaultages of France
Shall chide your trespass, and return your mock
In second accent of his ordnance.

DAUPHIN

Say, if my father render fair return,
It is against my will; for I desire
Nothing but odds with England: to that end,
As matching to his youth and vanity,
I did present him with the Paris balls.

EXETER

He'll make your Paris Louvre shake for it,
Were it the mistress-court of mighty Europe:
And, be assured, you'll find a difference,
As we, his subjects, have in wonder found,
Between the promise of his greener days
And these he masters now: now he weighs time,
Even to the utmost grain: — that you shall read
In your own losses, if he stay in France.

FRENCH KING

To-morrow shall you know our mind at full.

EXETER

Dispatch us with all speed, lest that our king

Come here himself to question our delay;
For he is footed in this land already.

FRENCH KING

You shall be soon dispatch'd with fair conditions:
A night is but small breath and little pause
To answer matters of this consequence.   *Flourish. Exeunt.*

ACT III

PROLOGUE

Enter CHORUS.

CHORUS

Thus with imagin'd wing our swift scene flies,
In motion of no less celerity
Than that of thought. Suppose that you have seen
The well-appointed king at Hampton pier
Embark his royalty; and his brave fleet
With silken streamers the young Phœbus fanning:
Play with your fancies; and in them behold
Upon the hempen tackle ship-boys climbing;
Hear the shrill whistle which doth order give
To sounds confus'd; behold the threaden sails,
Borne with th'invisible and creeping wind,
Draw the huge bottoms through the furrow'd sea,
Breasting the lofty surge: O, do but think
You stand upon the rivage, and behold
A city on th'inconstant billows dancing;
For so appears this fleet majestical,
Holding due course to Harfleur. Follow, follow!
Grapple your minds to sternage of this navy;
And leave your England, as dead midnight still,
Guarded with grandsires, babies, and old women,
Either past, or not arriv'd to, pith and puissance;
For who is he, whose chin is but enrich'd
With one appearing hair, that will not follow

These cull'd and choice-drawn cavaliers to France?
Work, work your thoughts, and therein see a siege;
Behold the ordnance on their carriages,
With fatal mouths gaping on girded Harfleur.
Suppose th'ambassador from the French comes back;
Tells Harry that the king doth offer him
Katharine his daughter; and with her, to dowry,
Some petty and unprofitable dukedoms.
The offer likes not: and the nimble gunner
With linstock now the devilish cannon touches,

                       [Alarum, and chambers go off, within.

And down goes all before them. Still be kind,
And eke out our performance with your mind.   *[Exit.*

SCENE I

France. Before Harfleur.

Alarums. Enter KING HENRY, EXETER, BEDFORD,
   GLOSTER, *and* SOLDIERS, *with scaling-ladders.*

KING HENRY

Once more unto the breach, dear friends, once more;
Or close the wall up with our English dead!
In peace there's nothing so becomes a man
As modest stillness and humility:
But when the blast of war blows in our ears,
Then imitate the action of the tiger;
Stiffen the sinews, summon up the blood,
Disguise fair nature with hard-favour'd rage:
Then lend the eye a terrible aspect;
Let it pry through the portage of the head
Like the brass cannon; let the brow o'erwhelm it
As fearfully as doth a galled rock
O'erhang and jutty his confounded base,
Swill'd with the wild and wasteful ocean.
Now set the teeth, and stretch the nostril wide;
Hold hard the breath, and bend up every spirit
To his full height! — On, on, you noble English,

Whose blood is fet from fathers of war-proof! —
Fathers that, like so many Alexanders,
Have in these parts from morn till even fought,
And sheath'd their swords for lack of argument: —
Dishonour not your mothers; now attest
That those whom you call'd fathers did beget you!
Be copy now to men of grosser blood,
And teach them how to war! — And you, good yeoman,
Whose limbs were made in England, show us here
The mettle of your pasture; let us swear
That you are worth your breeding: which I doubt not;
For there is none of you so mean and base,
That hath not noble lustre in your eyes.
I see you stand like greyhounds in the slips,
Straining upon the start. The game's afoot:
Follow your spirit; and, upon this charge,
Cry 'God for Harry, England, and Saint George!'
>   [*Exeunt. Alarum, and chambers go off, within.*

SCENE II

The same.
Enter NYM, BARDOLPH, PISTOL, *and* BOY.

BARDOLPH

On, on, on, on, on! to the breach, to the breach!

NYM

Pray thee, corporal, stay: the knocks are too hot; and,
for mine own part, I have not a case of lives: the humour
of it is too hot, that is the very plain-song of it.

PISTOL

The plain-song is most just; for humours do abound;
Knocks go and come; God's vassals drop and die;
>   And sword and shield,
>   In bloody field,
>   Doth win immortal fame.

BOY

Would I were in an alehouse in London! I would give all
my fame for a pot of ale and safety.

PISTOL

And I:

> If wishes would prevail with me,
> My purpose should not fail with me,
> But thither would I hie.

BOY

> As duly, but not as truly,
> As bird doth sing on bough.

Enter FLUELLEN.

FLUELLEN

God's plood! — Up to the preaches, you rascals! will
you not up to the preaches?   [*Driving them forward.*

PISTOL

Be merciful, great duke, to men of mould!
Abate thy rage, abate thy manly rage!
Abate thy rage, great duke!
Good bawcock, bate thy rage! use lenity, sweet chuck!

NYM

These be good humours! — your honour runs bad
humours.

[*Exeunt* NYM, BARDOLPH, *and* PISTOL, *driven in by*
FLUELLEN.

BOY

As young as I am, I have observed these three swashers.
I am boy to them all three: but all they three, though
they would serve me, could not be man to me; for,
indeed, three such antics do not amount to a man. For
Bardolph, — he is white-liver'd and red-faced; by the
means whereof a' faces it out, but fights not. For Pistol,
— he hath a killing tongue and a quiet sword; by the
means whereof a' break words, and keeps whole
weapons. For Nym, — he hath heard that men of few
words are the best men; and therefore he scorns to say
his prayers, lest a' should be thought a coward: but his

few bad words are match'd with as few good deeds; for
a' never broke any man's head but his own, and that was
against a post when he was drunk. They will steal any
thing, and call it purchase. Bardolph stole a lute-case,
bore it twelve leagues, and sold it for three-half-pence.
Nym and Bardolph are sworn brothers in filching; and
in Calais they stole a fire-shovel: I knew by that piece of
service the men would carry coals. They would have me
as familiar with men's pockets as their gloves or their
handkerchers: which makes much against my manhood,
if I should take from another's pocket to put into mine;
for it is plain pocketing-up of wrongs. I must leave them,
and seek some better service: their villainy goes against
my weak stomach, and therefore I must cast it up.

[*Exit.*

Enter FLUELLEN, GOWER *following.*

GOWER

Captain Fluellen, you must come presently to the
mines; the Duke of Gloster would speak with you.

FLUELLEN

To the mines! tell you the duke, it is not so good to
come to the mines; for, look you, the mines is not
according to the disciplines of the war: the concavities of
it is not sufficient; for, look you, th'athversary — you
may discuss unto the duke, look you — is digg'd himself
four yard under the countermines: by Cheshu, I think a'
will plough up all, if there is not petter directions.

GOWER

The Duke of Gloster, to whom the order of the siege is
given, is altogether directed by an Irishman, — a very
valiant gentleman, i'faith.

FLUELLEN

It is Captain Macmorris, is it not?

GOWER

I think it be.

FLUELLEN

By Cheshu, he is an ass, as in the 'orld: I will verify as
much in his peard: he has no more directions in the true
disciplines of the wars, look you, of the Roman
disciplines, than is a puppy-dog.

GOWER

Here a' comes; and the Scots captain, Captain Jamy,
with him.

FLUELLEN

Captain Jamy is a marvellous falorous gentleman, that is
certain; and of great expedition and knowledge in
th'auncient wars, upon my particular knowledge of his
directions: by Cheshu, he will maintain his argument as
well as any military man in the 'orld, in the disciplines of
the pristine wars of the Romans.

Enter MACMORRIS *and* JAMY.

JAMY

I say gude-day, Captain Fluellen.

FLUELLEN

Got-den to your worship, goot Captain Jamy.

GOWER

How now, Captain Macmorris! have you quit the
mines? have the pioners given o'er?

MACMORRIS

By Chrish, la, tish ill done; the work ish give over, the
trompet sound the retreat. By my hand, I swear, and my
father's soul, the work ish ill done; it ish give over: I
would have blow'd up the town, so Chrish save me, la,
in an hour: O, tish ill done, tish ill done; by my hand,
tish ill done!

FLUELLEN

Captain Macmorris, I peseech you now, will you
voutsafe me, look you, a few disputations with you, as
partly touching or concerning the disciplines of the war,
the Roman wars, in the way of argument, look you, and
friendly communication; partly to satisfy my opinion,

and partly for the satisfaction, look you, of my mind, as
touching the direction of the military discipline; that is
the point.

JAMY

It sall be vary gude, gude feith, gud captains baith: and I
sall quit you with gude leve, as I may pick occasion; that
sall I, marry.

MACMORRIS

It is no time to discourse, so Chrish save me: the day is
hot, and the weather, and the wars, and the king, and
the dukes: it is no time to discourse. The town is
beseech'd, and the trompet call us to the breach; and we
talk, and, be Chrish, do nothing: 'tis shame for us all: so
God sa' me, 'tis shame to stand still; it is shame, by my
hand: and there is throats to be cut, and works to be
done; and there ish nothing done, so Chrish sa' me, la.

JAMY

By the mess, ere theise eyes of mine take themselves to
slomber, ay'll de gude service, or ay'll lig i'th'grund for
it; ay, or go to death; and ay'll pay't as valorously as I
may, that sall I suerly do, that is the breff and the long.
Marry, I wad full fain heard some question 'tween you
tway.

FLUELLEN

Captain Macmorris, I think, look you, under your
correction, there is not many of your nation —

MACMORRIS

Of my nation! What ish my nation? Ish a villain, and a
bastard, and a knave, and a rascal. What ish my nation?
Who talks of my nation?

FLUELLEN

Look you, if you take the matter otherwise than is
meant, Captain Macmorris, peradventure I shall think
you do not use me with that affability as in discretion
you ought to use me, look you; being as goot a man as
yourself, both in the disciplines of war, and in the
derivation of my birth, and in other particularities.

MACMORRIS

I do not know you so good a man as myself: so Chrish
save me, I will cut off your head.

GOWER

Gentlemen both, you will mistake each other.

JAMY

A! that's a foul fault.   [*A parley sounded.*

GOWER

The town sounds a parley.

FLUELLEN

Captain Macmorris, when there is more petter
opportunity to be required, look you, I will be so pold as
to tell you I know the disciplines of war; and there is an
end.   [*Exeunt.*

SCENE III

The same.

The GOVERNOR *and some* CITIZENS *on the walls; the
English forces below. Enter* KING HENRY *and his* TRAIN
before the gates.

KING HENRY

How yet resolves the governor of the town?
This is the latest parle we will admit:
Therefore, to our best mercy give yourselves;
Or, like to men proud of destruction,
Defy us to our worst: for, as I am a soldier,
A name that, in my thoughts, becomes me best,
If I begin the battery once again,
I will not leave the half-achiev'd Harfleur
Till in her ashes she lie buried.
The gates of mercy shall be all shut up;
And the flesh'd soldier, — rough and hard of heart, —
In liberty of bloody hand shall range
With conscience wide as hell; mowing like grass
Your fresh-fair virgins and your flowering infants.

What is it then to me, if impious war, —
Array'd in flames, like to the prince of fiends, —
Do, with his smirch'd complexion, all fell feats
Enlink'd to waste and desolation?
What is't to me, when you yourselves are cause,
If your pure maidens fall into the hand
Of hot and forcing violation?
What rein can hold licentious wickedness
When down the hill he holds his fierce career?
We may as bootless spend our vain command
Upon th'enraged soldiers in their spoil,
As send precepts to the leviathan
To come ashore. Therefore, you men of Harfleur,
Take pity of your town and of your people,
Whiles yet my soldiers are in my command;
Whiles yet the cool and temperate wind of grace
O'erblows the filthy and contagious clouds
Of heady murder, spoil, and villainy.
If not, why, in a moment, look to see
The blind and bloody soldier with foul hand
Defile the locks of your shrill-shrieking daughters;
Your fathers taken by the silver beards,
And their most reverend heads dash'd to the walls;
Your naked infants spitted upon pikes,
Whiles the mad mothers with their howls confused
Do break the clouds, as did the wives of Jewry
At Herod's bloody-hunting slaughtermen.
What say you? will you yield, and this avoid?
Or, guilty in defence, be thus destroy'd?

GOVERNOR OF HARFLEUR

Our expectation hath this day an end:
The Dauphin, whom of succour we entreated,
Returns us, that his powers are yet not ready
To raise so great a siege. Therefore, dread king,
We yield our town and lives to thy soft mercy.
Enter our gates; dispose of us and ours;
For we no longer are defensible.

KING HENRY

Open your gates. — Come, uncle Exeter,
Go you and enter Harfleur; there remain,
And fortify it strongly 'gainst the French:
Use mercy to them all. For us, dear uncle, —
The winter coming on, and sickness growing
Upon our soldiers, — we will retire to Calais.
To-night in Harfleur will we be your guest;
To-morrow for the march are we address'd.

[Flourish, and enter the town.

SCENE IV

The French KING'S palace.
Enter KATHARINE and ALICE.

KATHARINE

Alice, tu as été en Angleterre, et tu parles bien le langage.

ALICE

Un peu, madame.

KATHARINE

Je te prie, m'enseignez; il faut que j'apprenne à parler.
Comment appelez-vous la main en Anglois?

ALICE

La main? elle est appelée de hand.

KATHARINE

De hand. *Et les doigts?*

ALICE

Les doigts? ma foi, j'oublie les doigts; mais je me souviendrai.
Les doigts? je pense qu'ils sont appelés de fingres; *oui, de*
fingres.

KATHARINE

La main, de hand; *les doigts, de* fingres. *Je pense que je suis*
le bon écolier; j'ai gagné deux mots d'Anglois vitement.
Comment appelez-vous les ongles?

ALICE

Les ongles? nous les appelons de nails.

KATHARINE

De nails. *Ecoutez; dites-moi, si je parle bien:* de hand, de fingres, *et* de nails.

ALICE

C'est bien dit, madame; il est fort bon Anglois.

KATHARINE

Dites-moi l'Anglois pour le bras.

ALICE

De arm, *madame.*

KATHARINE

Et le coude?

ALICE

D'elbow.

KATHARINE

D'elbow. *Je m'en fais la répétition de tous les mots que vous m'avez appris dès à présent.*

ALICE

Il est trop difficile, madame, comme je pense.

KATHARINE

Excusez-moi, Alice; écoutez: d'hand, de fingres, de nails, d'arm, de bilbow.

ALICE

D'elbow, *madame.*

KATHARINE

O Seigneur Dieu, je m'en oublie! d'elbow. *Comment appelez-vous le col?*

ALICE

De neck, *madame.*

KATHARINE

De nick. *Et le menton?*

ALICE

De chin.

KATHARINE

De sin. *Le col,* de nick; *le menton,* de sin.

ALICE

Oui. Sauf votre honneur, en vérité, vous prononcez les mots aussi droit que les natifs d'Angleterre.

KATHARINE

Je ne doute point d'apprendre, par la grace de Dieu, et en peu de temps.

ALICE

N'avez-vous pas déjà oublié ce que je vous ai enseigné?

KATHARINE

Non, je réciterai à vous promptement: d'hand, de fingres, de mails, —

ALICE

De nails, *madame.*

KATHARINE

De nails, de arm, de ilbow.

ALICE

Sauf votre honneur, d'elbow.

KATHARINE

Ainsi dis-je; d'elbow, de nick, *et* de sin. *Comment appelez-vous le pied et la robe?*

ALICE

De foot, *madame; et* de coun.

KATHARINE

De foot *et de* coun! *O Seigneur Dieu! ce sont mots de son mauvais, corruptible, gros, et impudique, et non pour les dames d'honneur d'user: je ne voudrais prononcer ces mots devant les seigneurs de France pour tout le monde. Foh! le* foot *et le* coun! *Néanmoins, je réciterai une autre fois ma leçon ensemble:* d'hand, de fingres, de nails, d'arm, d'elbow, de nick, de sin, de foot, de coun.

ALICE

Excellent, madame!

KATHARINE

C'est assez pour une fois: allons-nous à diner. [*Exeunt.*

49

SCENE V

The same.

Enter the KING OF FRANCE, the DAUPHIN,
    BOURBON, the CONSTABLE OF FRANCE, and
    others.

FRENCH KING

'Tis certain he hath pass'd the river Somme.

CONSTABLE

And if he be not fought withal, my lord,
Let us not live in France; let us quit all,
And give our vineyards to a barbarous people.

DAUPHIN

O *Dieu vivant!* hall a few sprays of us,
The emptying of our fathers' luxury,
Our scions, put in wild and savage stock,
Spirit up so suddenly into the clouds,
And overlook their grafters?

BOURBON

Normans, but bastard Normans, Norman bastards!
Mort de ma vie! if they march along
Unfought withal, but I will sell my dukedom,
To buy a slobbery and a dirty farm
In that nook-shotten isle of Albion.

CONSTABLE

Dieu de batailles! where have they this mettle?
Is not their climate foggy, raw, and dull;
On whom, as in despite, the sun looks pale,
Killing their fruit with frowns? Can sodden water,
A drench for sur-rein'd jades, their barley-broth,
Decoct their cold blood to such valiant heat?
And shall our quick blood, spirited with wine,
Seem frosty? O, for honour of our land,
Let us not hang like roping icicles
Upon our houses' thatch, whiles a more frosty people
Sweat drops of gallant youth in our rich fields, —
Poor we may call them in their native lords!

DAUPHIN

By faith and honour,
Our madams mock at us, and plainly say
Our mettle is bred out, and they will give
Their bodies to the lust of English youth
To new-store France with bastard warriors.

BOURBON

They bid us to the English dancing-schools,
And teach lavoltas high and swift corantos;
Saying our grace is only in our heels,
And that we are most lofty runaways.

FRENCH KING

Where is Montjoy the herald? speed him hence;
Let him greet England with our sharp defiance. —
Up, princes! and, with spirit of honour edged
More sharper than your swords, hie to the field:
Charles Delabreth, high-Constable of France;
You Dukes of Orleans, Bourbon, and of Berri,
Alençon, Brabant, Bar, and Burgundy;
Jaques Chatillon, Rambures, Vaudemont,
Beaumont, Grandpré, Roussi, and Fauconberg,
Foix, Lestrale, Bouciqualt, and Charolois;
High dukes, great princes, barons, lords, and knights,
For your great seats now quit you of great shames.
Bar Harry England, that sweeps through our land
With pennons painted in the blood of Harfleur:
Rush on his host, as doth the melted snow
Upon the valleys, whose low vassal seat
The Alps doth spit and void his rheum upon:
Go down upon him, — you have power enough, —
And in a captive chariot into Rouen
Bring him our prisoner.

CONSTABLE

              This becomes the great.
Sorry am I his numbers are so few,
His soldiers sick, and famish'd in their march;
For I am sure, when he shall see our army,

He'll drop his heart into the sink of fear,
And for achievement offer us his ransom.

FRENCH KING

Therefore, lord Constable, haste on Montjoy;
And let him say to England, that we send
To know what willing ransom he will give. —
Prince Dauphin, you shall stay with us in Rouen.

DAUPHIN

Not so, I do beseech your majesty.

FRENCH KING

Be patient; for you shall remain with us.
Now forth, lord Constable, and princes all,
And quickly bring us word of England's fall.   [*Exeunt.*

SCENE VI

The English camp in Picardy.
Enter GOWER and FLUELLEN, *meeting.*

GOWER

How now, Captain Fluellen! come you from the bridge?

FLUELLEN

I assure you, there is very excellent services committed
at the pridge.

GOWER

Is the Duke of Exeter safe?

FLUELLEN

The Duke of Exeter is as magnanimous as Agamemnon;
and a man that I love and honour with my soul, and my
heart, and my duty, and my life, and my living, and my
uttermost power: he is not — Got be praised and plest!
— any hurt in the 'orld; but keeps the pridge most
valiantly, with excellent discipline. There is an auncient
there at the pridge, — I think in my very conscience he
is as valiant a man as Mark Antony; and he is a man of
no estimation in the 'orld; but I did see him do gallant
service.

GOWER

What do you call him?

FLUELLEN

He is called Auncient Pistol.

GOWER

I know him not.

FLUELLEN

Here is the man.

Enter PISTOL.

PISTOL

Captain, I thee beseech to do me favours:
The Duke of Exeter doth love thee well.

FLUELLEN

Ay, I praise Got; and I have merited some love at his
hands.

PISTOL

Bardolph, a soldier, firm and sound of heart,
And of buxom valour, hath, by cruel fate,
And giddy Fortune's furious fickle wheel, —
That goddess blind,
That stands upon the rolling restless stone, —

FLUELLEN

By your patience, Auncient Pistol. Fortune is painted
plind, with a muffler afore her eyes, to signify to you
that Fortune is plind; and she is painted also with a
wheel, to signify to you, which is the moral of it, that she
is turning, and inconstant, and mutability, and variation:
and her foot, look you, is fix'd upon a spherical stone,
which rolls, and rolls, and rolls: — in good truth, the
poet makes a most excellent description of it: Fortune is
an excellent moral.

PISTOL

Fortune is Bardolph's foe, and frowns on him;
For he hath stol'n a pax, and hanged must a' be, —
A damned death!
Let gallows gape for dog; let man go free,

And let not hemp his windpipe suffocate:
But Exeter hath given the doom of death
For pax of little price.
Therefore, go speak, — the duke will hear thy voice;
And let not Bardolph's vital thread be cut
With edge of penny cord and vile reproach:
Speak, captain, for his life, and I will thee requite.

FLUELLEN

Auncient Pistol, I do partly understand your meaning.

PISTOL

Why, then, rejoice therefore.

FLUELLEN

Certainly, auncient, it is not a thing to rejoice at: for if,
look you, he were my prother, I would desire the duke
to use his goot pleasure, and put him to execution; for
discipline ought to be used.

PISTOL

Die and be damn'd! and figo for thy friendship!

FLUELLEN

It is well.

PISTOL

The fig of Spain!   [*Exit.*

FLUELLEN

Very goot.

GOWER

Why, this is an arrant counterfeit rascal; I remember
him now; a bawd, a cutpurse.

FLUELLEN

I'll assure you, a' utter'd as prave 'ords at the pridge as
you shall see in a summer's day. But it is very well; what
he has spoke to me, that is well, I warrant you, when
time is serve.

GOWER

Why, 'tis a gull, a fool, a rogue, that now and then goes
to the wars, to grace himself, at his return into London,
under the form of a soldier. And such fellows are perfect

in the great commanders' names: and they will learn you
by rote where services were done; — at such and such a
sconce, at such a breach, at such a convoy; who came
off bravely, who was shot, who disgraced, what terms
the enemy stood on; and this they con perfectly in the
phrase of war, which they trick up with new-turn'd
oaths: and what a beard of the general's cut, and a
horrid suit of the camp, will do among foaming bottles
and ale-wash'd wits, is wonderful to be thought on. But
you must learn to know such slanders of the age, or else
you may be marvellously mistook.

FLUELLEN

I tell you what, Captain Gower; — I do perceive he is
not the man that he would gladly make show to the 'orld
he is: if I find a hole in his coat, I will tell him my mind.
[*Drum within.*] Hark you, the king is coming; and I must
speak with him from the pridge.

Drum and colours. Enter KING HENRY, GLOSTER, *and
his poor* SOLDIERS.

Got pless your majesty!

KING HENRY

How now, Fluellen! camest thou from the bridge?

FLUELLEN

Ay, so please your majesty. The Duke of Exeter has very
gallantly maintain'd the pridge: the French is gone off,
look you; and there is gallant and most prave passages:
marry, th'athversary was have possession of the pridge;
but he is enforced to retire, and the Duke of Exeter is
master of the pridge: I can tell your majesty, the duke is
a prave man.

KING HENRY

What men have you lost, Fluellen?

FLUELLEN

The perdition of th'athversary hath been very great,
reasonable great: marry, for my part, I think the duke
hath lost never a man, but one that is like to be executed
for robbing a church, — one Bardolph, if your majesty

know the man: his face is all bubukles, and whelks, and
knobs, and flames o' fire: and his lips plows at his nose,
and it is like a coal of fire, sometimes plue and sometimes
red; but his nose is executed, and his fire's out.

KING HENRY

We would have all such offenders so cut off: — and we
give express charge that, in our marches through the
country, there be nothing compell'd from the villages,
nothing taken but paid for, none of the French
upbraided or abused in disdainful language; for when
lenity and cruelty play for a kingdom, the gentler
gamester is the soonest winner.

Tucket. Enter MONTJOY.

MONTJOY

You know me by my habit.

KING HENRY

Well, then, I know thee: what shall I know of thee?

MONTJOY

My master's mind.

KING HENRY

Unfold it.

MONTJOY

Thus says my king: — Say thou to Harry of England:
Though we seem'd dead, we did but sleep; advantage is
a better soldier than rashness. Tell him, we could have
rebuked him at Harfleur, but that we thought not good
to bruise an injury till it were full ripe: — now we speak
upon our cue, and our voice is imperial: England shall
repent his folly, see his weakness, and admire our
sufferance. Bid him, therefore, consider of his ransom;
which must proportion the losses we have borne, the
subjects we have lost, the disgrace we have digested;
which, in weight to re-answer, his pettiness would bow
under. For our losses, his exchequer is too poor; for
th'effusion of our blood, the muster of his kingdom too
faint a number, and for our disgrace, his own person,
kneeling at our feet, but a weak and worthless

satisfaction. To this add defiance: and tell him, for
conclusion, he hath betray'd his followers, whose
condemnation is pronounced. So far my king and
master; so much my office.

KING HENRY

What is thy name? I know thy quality.

MONTJOY

Montjoy.

KING HENRY

Thou dost thy office fairly. Turn thee back,
And tell thy king, — I do not seek him now;
But could be willing to march on to Calais
Without impeachment: for, to say the sooth, —
Though 'tis no wisdom to confess so much
Unto an enemy of craft and vantage, —
My people are with sickness much enfeebled;
My numbers lessen'd; and those few I have,
Almost no better than so many French;
Who when they were in health, I tell thee, herald,
I thought upon one pair of English legs
Did march three Frenchmen. — Yet, forgive me, God,
That I do brag thus! — this your air of France
Hath blown that vice in me; I must repent.
Go, therefore, tell thy master here I am;
My ransom is this frail and worthless trunk;
My army but a weak and sickly guard:
Yet, God before, tell him we will come on,
Though France himself, and such another neighbour,
Stand in our way. There's for thy labour, Montjoy.

[*Gives a purse.*

Go, bid thy master well advise himself:
If we may pass, we will; if we be hinder'd,
We shall your tawny ground with your red blood
Discolour: and so, Montjoy, fare you well.
The sum of all our answer is but this:
We would not seek a battle, as we are;
Nor, as we are, we say, we will not shun it:

So tell your master.

MONTJOY

I shall deliver so. Thanks to your highness.   [*Exit.*

GLOSTER

I hope they will not come upon us now.

KING HENRY

We are in God's hand, brother, not in theirs.
March to the bridge; it now draws toward night: —
Beyond the river we'll encamp ourselves;
And on to-morrow bid them march away.   [*Exeunt.*

SCENE VII

The French camp near Agincourt.

Enter the CONSTABLE OF FRANCE, *the* LORD
RAMBURES, ORLEANS, *the* DAUPHIN, *and others.*

CONSTABLE

Tut! I have the best armour of the world. — Would it
were day!

ORLEANS

You have an excellent armour; but let my horse have his
due.

CONSTABLE

It is the best horse of Europe.

ORLEANS

Will it never be morning?

DAUPHIN

My Lord of Orleans, and my lord high-Constable, you
talk of horse and armour?

ORLEANS

You are as well provided of both as any prince in the
world.

DAUPHIN

What a long night is this! — I will not change my horse
with any that treads but on four pasterns. *Ca, ha!* he
bounds from the earth, as if his entrails were hairs; *le*

cheval volant, the Pegasus, *qui a les narines de feu!* When I
bestride him, I soar, I am a hawk: he trots the air; the
earth sings when he touches it; the basest horn of his
hoof is more musical than the pipe of Hermes.

ORLEANS

He's of the colour of the nutmeg.

DAUPHIN

And of the heat of the ginger. It is a beast for Perseus:
he is pure air and fire; and the dull elements of earth
and water never appear in him, but only in patient
stillness while his rider mounts him: he is, indeed, a
horse; and all other jades you may call beasts.

CONSTABLE

Indeed, my lord, it is a most absolute and excellent horse.

DAUPHIN

It is the prince of palfreys; his neigh is like the bidding of
a monarch, and his countenance enforces homage.

ORLEANS

No more, cousin.

DAUPHIN

Nay, the man hath no wit that cannot, from the rising of
the lark to the lodging of the lamb, vary deserved praise on
my palfrey: it is a theme as fluent as the sea; turn the sands
into eloquent tongues, and my horse is argument for them
all: 'tis a subject for a sovereign to reason on, and for a
sovereign's sovereign to ride on; and for the world, familiar
to us and unknown, to lay apart their particular functions,
and wonder at him. I once writ a sonnet in his praise, and
began thus: 'Wonder of nature,' —

ORLEANS

I have heard a sonnet begin so to one's mistress.

DAUPHIN

Then did they imitate that which I composed to my
courser; for my horse is my mistress.

ORLEANS

Your mistress bears well.

DAUPHIN

Me well; which is the prescript praise and perfection of a
good and particular mistress.

CONSTABLE

Ma foi, methought yesterday your mistress shrewdly
shook your back.

DAUPHIN

So, perhaps, did yours.

CONSTABLE

Mine was not bridled.

DAUPHIN

O, then, belike she was old and gentle; and you rode,
like a kern of Ireland, your French hose off, and in your
strait strossers.

CONSTABLE

You have good judgement in horsemanship.

DAUPHIN

Be warn'd by me, then: they that ride so, and ride not
warily, fall into foul bogs. I had rather have my horse to
my mistress.

CONSTABLE

I had as lief have my mistress a jade.

DAUPHIN

I tell thee, Constable, my mistress wears his own hair.

CONSTABLE

I could make as true a boast as that, if I had a sow to my
mistress.

DAUPHIN

*Le chien est retourné à son propre vomissement, et la truie
lavée au bourbier*: thou makest use of any thing.

CONSTABLE

Yet do I not use my horse for my mistress; or any such
proverb, so little kin to the purpose.

RAMBURES

My lord Constable, the armour that I saw in your tent
to-night, — are those stars or suns upon it?

CONSTABLE
Stars, my lord.

DAUPHIN
Some of them will fall to-morrow, I hope.

CONSTABLE
And yet my sky shall not want.

DAUPHIN
That may be, for you bear a many superfluously, and
'twere more honour some were away.

CONSTABLE
Even as your horse bears your praises; who would trot as
well, were some of your brags dismounted.

DAUPHIN
Would I were able to load him with his desert! — Will it
never be day? — I will trot to-morrow a mile, and my
way shall be paved with English faces.

CONSTABLE
I will not say so, for fear I should be faced out of my
way: but I would it were morning; for I would fain be
about the ears of the English.

RAMBURES
Who will go to hazard with me for twenty prisoners?

CONSTABLE
You must first go yourself to hazard, ere you have them.

DAUPHIN
'Tis midnight; I'll go arm myself.   [*Exit.*

ORLEANS
The Dauphin longs for morning.

RAMBURES
He longs to eat the English.

CONSTABLE
I think he will eat all he kills.

ORLEANS
By the white hand of my lady, he's a gallant prince.

CONSTABLE
Swear by her foot, that she may tread out the oath.

ORLEANS

He is, simply, the most active gentleman of France.

CONSTABLE

Doing is activity; and he will still be doing.

ORLEANS

He never did harm, that I heard of.

CONSTABLE

Nor will do none to-morrow: he will keep that good name still.

ORLEANS

I know him to be valiant.

CONSTABLE

I was told that by one that knows him better than you.

ORLEANS

What's he?

CONSTABLE

Marry, he told me so himself; and he said he cared not who knew it.

ORLEANS

He needs not; it is no hidden virtue in him.

CONSTABLE

By my faith, sir, but it is; never any body saw it but his lackey: 'tis a hooded valour; and when it appears, it will bate.

ORLEANS

Ill-will never said well.

CONSTABLE

I will cap that proverb with — There is flattery in friendship.

ORLEANS

And I will take up that with — Give the devil his due.

CONSTABLE

Well placed: there stands your friend for the devil: have at the very eye of that proverb, with — A pox of the devil.

ORLEANS

You are the better at proverbs, by how much — A fool's
bolt is soon shot.

CONSTABLE

You have shot over.

ORLEANS

'Tis not the first time you were overshot.

Enter a MESSENGER.

MESSENGER

My lord high-Constable, the English lie within fifteen
hundred paces of your tents.

CONSTABLE

Who hath measured the ground?

MESSENGER

The Lord Grandpré.

CONSTABLE

A valiant and most expert gentleman. — Would it were
day! — Alas, poor Harry of England! he longs not for
the dawning, as we do.

ORLEANS

What a wretched and peevish fellow is this king of
England, to mope with his fat-brain'd followers so far
out of his knowledge!

CONSTABLE

If the English had any apprehension, they would run away.

ORLEANS

That they lack; for if their heads had any intellectual
armour, they could never wear such heavy head-pieces.

RAMBURES

That island of England breeds very valiant creatures;
their mastiffs are of unmatchable courage.

ORLEANS

Foolish curs, that run winking into the mouth of a
Russian bear, and have their heads crush'd like rotten
apples! You may as well say, that's a valiant flea that
dare eat his breakfast on the lip of a lion.

CONSTABLE

Just, just; and the men do sympathise with the mastiffs
in robustious and rough coming-on, leaving their wits
with their wives: and then give them great meals of beef,
and iron and steel, they will eat like wolves, and fight
like devils.

ORLEANS

Ay, but these English are shrewdly out of beef.

CONSTABLE

Then shall we find to-morrow they have only stomachs
to eat, and none to fight. Now is it time to arm: come,
shall we about it?

ORLEANS

It is now two o'clock: but, let me see, — by ten
We shall have each a hundred Englishmen.   [*Exeunt.*

ACT IV

PROLOGUE

Enter CHORUS.

CHORUS

Now entertain conjecture of a time
When creeping murmur and the poring dark
Fills the wide vessel of the universe.
From camp to camp, through the foul womb of night,
The hum of either army stilly sounds,
That the fix'd sentinels almost receive
The secret whispers of each other's watch:
Fire answers fire; and through their paly flames
Each battle sees the other's umber'd face:
Steed threatens steed, in high and boastful neighs
Piercing the night's dull ear; and from the tents,
The armourers, accomplishing the knights,
With busy hammers closing rivets up,
Give dreadful note of preparation:

The country cocks do crow, the clocks do toll,
And the third hour of drowsy morning name.
Proud of their numbers, and secure in soul,
The confident and over-lusty French
Do the low-rated English play at dice;
And chide the cripple tardy-gaited night,
Who, like a foul and ugly witch, doth limp
So tediously away. The poor condemned English,
Like sacrifices, by their watchful fires
Sit patiently, and inly ruminate
The morning's danger; and their gesture sad
Investing lank-lean cheeks, and war-worn coats,
Presenteth them unto the gazing moon
So many horrid ghosts. O, now, who will behold
The royal captain of this ruin'd band
Walking from watch to watch, from tent to tent,
Let him cry, 'Praise and glory on his head!'
For forth he goes and visits all his host;
Bids them good morrow with a modest smile,
And calls them brothers, friends, and countrymen.
Upon his royal face there is no note
How dread an army hath enrounded him;
Nor doth he dedicate one jot of colour
Unto the weary and all-watched night,
But freshly looks, and over-bears attaint
With cheerful semblance and sweet majesty;
That every wretch, pining and pale before,
Beholding him, plucks comfort from his looks:
A largess universal, like the sun,
His liberal eye doth give to every one,
Thawing cold fear. Then, mean and gentle all,
Behold, as may unworthiness define,
A little touch of Harry in the night:
And so our scene must to the battle fly;
Where — O for pity! — we shall much disgrace
With four or five most vile and ragged foils,
Right ill-dispos'd, in brawl ridiculous,

The name of Agincourt. Yet, sit and see;
Minding true things by what their mockeries be.   [*Exit.*

SCENE I

The English camp at Agincourt.
Enter KING HENRY, BEDFORD, and GLOSTER.

KING HENRY

Gloster, 'tis true that we are in great danger;
The greater therefore should our courage be. —
Good morrow, brother Bedford. — God Almighty!
There is some soul of goodness in things evil,
Would men observingly distil it out;
For our bad neighbour makes us early stirrers,
Which is both healthful and good husbandry:
Besides, they are our outward consciences,
And preachers to us all; admonishing
That we should dress us fairly for our end.
Thus may we gather honey from the weed,
And make a moral of the devil himself.
                    Enter ERPINGHAM.
Good morrow, old Sir Thomas Erpingham:
A good soft pillow for that good white head
Were better than a churlish turf of France.

ERPINGHAM

Not so, my liege: this lodging likes me better,
Since I may say, 'Now lie I like a king.'

KING HENRY

'Tis good for men to love their present pains
Upon example; so the spirit is eased:
And when the mind is quicken'd, out of doubt
The organs, though defunct and dead before,
Break up their drowsy grave, and newly move
With casted slough and fresh legerity.
Lend me thy cloak, Sir Thomas. — Brothers both,
Commend me to the princes in our camp;
Do my good morrow to them; and anon

Desire them all to my pavilion.

GLOSTER

We shall, my liege.

ERPINGHAM

Shall I attend your Grace?

KING HENRY

               No, my good knight;
Go with my brothers to my lords of England:
I and my bosom must debate awhile,
And then I would no other company.

ERPINGHAM

The Lord in heaven bless thee, noble Harry!

[*Exeunt* GLOSTER, BEDFORD, *and* ERPINGHAM.

KING HENRY

God-a-mercy, old heart! thou speak'st cheerfully.

Enter PISTOL.

PISTOL

Qui va là?

KING HENRY

A friend.

PISTOL

Discuss unto me; art thou officer?
Or art thou base, common, and popular?

KING HENRY

I am a gentleman of a company.

PISTOL

Trail'st thou the puissant pike?

KING HENRY

Even so. What are you?

PISTOL

As good a gentleman as the emperor.

KING HENRY

Then you are a better than the king.

PISTOL

The king's a bawcock, and a heart of gold,
A lad of life, an imp of fame;

Of parents good, of fist most valiant:
I kiss his dirty shoe, and from heart-string
I love the lovely bully. — What is thy name?

KING HENRY

Harry *le Roy*.

PISTOL

Le Roy!
A Cornish name: art thou of Cornish crew?

KING HENRY

No, I am a Welshman.

PISTOL

Know'st thou Fluellen?

KING HENRY

Yes.

PISTOL

Tell him, I'll knock his leek about his pate
Upon Saint Davy's day.

KING HENRY

Do not you wear your dagger in your cap that day, lest
he knock that about yours.

PISTOL

Art thou his friend?

KING HENRY

And his kinsman too.

PISTOL

The figo for thee, then!

KING HENRY

I thank you: God be with you!

PISTOL

My name is Pistol call'd. [*Exit.*

KING HENRY

It sorts well with your fierceness.

   Enter FLUELLEN *and* GOWER, *severally.*

GOWER

Captain Fluellen!

FLUELLEN

So! in the name of Cheshu Christ, speak lower. It is the
greatest admiration of the universal 'orld, when the true
and auncient prerogatifs and laws of the wars is not kept:
if you would take the pains but to examine the wars of
Pompey the Great, you shall find, I warrant you, that
there is no tiddle-taddle nor pibble-pabble in Pompey's
camp; I warrant you, you shall find the ceremonies of the
wars, and the cares of it, and the forms of it, and the
sobriety of it, and the modesty of it, to be otherwise.

GOWER

Why, the enemy is loud; you heard him all night.

FLUELLEN

If the enemy is an ass, and a fool, and a prating
coxcomb, is it meet, think you, that we should also, look
you, be an ass, and a fool, and a prating coxcomb, — in
your own conscience, now?

GOWER

I will speak lower.

FLUELLEN

I pray you, and peseech you, that you will.

[*Exeunt* GOWER *and* FLUELLEN.

KING HENRY

Though it appear a little out of fashion,
There is much care and valour in this Welshman.

Enter three SOLDIERS, JOHN BATES, ALEXANDER
COURT, *and* MICHAEL WILLIAMS.

ALEXANDER COURT

Brother John Bates, is not that the morning which
breaks yonder?

JOHN BATES

I think it be: but we have no great cause to desire the
approach of day.

MICHAEL WILLIAMS

We see yonder the beginning of the day, but I think
we shall never see the end of it. — Who goes there?

KING HENRY

A friend.

MICHAEL WILLIAMS

Under what captain serve you?

KING HENRY

Under Sir Thomas Erpingham.

MICHAEL WILLIAMS

A good old commander and a most kind gentleman: I
pray you, what thinks he of our estate?

KING HENRY

Even as men wreck'd upon a sand, that look to be
wash'd off the next tide.

JOHN BATES

He hath not told his thought to the king?

KING HENRY

No; nor is it meet he should. For, though I speak it to
you, I think the king is but a man, as I am: the violet
smells to him as it doth to me; the element shows to him
as it doth to me; all his senses have but human
conditions: his ceremonies laid by, in his nakedness he
appears but a man; and though his affections are higher
mounted than ours, yet, when they stoop, they stoop
with the like wing. Therefore when he sees reason of
fears, as we do, his fears, out of doubt, be of the same
relish as ours are: yet, in reason, no man should possess
him with any appearance of fear, lest he, by showing it,
should dishearten his army.

JOHN BATES

He may show what outward courage he will; but I
believe, as cold a night as 'tis, he could wish himself in
Thames up to the neck; — and so I would he were, and
I by him, at all adventures, so we were quit here.

KING HENRY

By my troth, I will speak my conscience of the king: I think
he would not wish himself any where but where he is.

JOHN BATES

Then I would he were here alone; so should he be sure
to be ransom'd, and a many poor men's lives saved.

KING HENRY

I dare say you love him not so ill, to wish him here
alone, howsoever you speak this, to feel other men's
minds: methinks I could not die any where so contented
as in the king's company, — his cause being just, and his
quarrel honourable.

MICHAEL WILLIAMS

That's more than we know.

JOHN BATES

Ay, or more than we should seek after; for we know
enough, if we know we are the king's subjects: if his
cause be wrong, our obedience to the king wipes the
crime of it out of us.

MICHAEL WILLIAMS

But if the cause be not good, the king himself hath a
heavy reckoning to make, when all those legs and arms
and heads, chopp'd off in battle, shall join together at
the latter day, and cry all, 'We died at such a place';
some swearing; some crying for a surgeon; some, upon
their wives left poor behind them; some, upon the debts
they owe; some, upon their children rawly left. I am
afeard there are few die well that die in battle, for how
can they charitably dispose of any thing, when blood is
their argument? Now, if these men do not die well, it
will be a black matter for the king that led them to it;
who to disobey were against all proportion of subjection.

KING HENRY

So, if a son, that is by his father sent about merchandise,
do sinfully miscarry upon the sea, the imputation of his
wickedness, by your rule, should be imposed upon his
father that sent him: or if a servant, under his master's
command transporting a sum of money, be assail'd by
robbers, and die in many irreconciled iniquities, you
may call the business of the master the author of the

servant's damnation: — but this is not so: the king is not bound to answer the particular endings of his soldiers, the father of his son, nor the master of his servant; for they purpose not their death, when they purpose their services. Besides, there is no king, be his cause never so spotless, if it come to the arbitrement of swords, can try it out with all unspotted soldiers: some peradventure have on them the guilt of premeditated and contrived murder; some, of beguiling virgins with the broken seals of perjury; some, making the wars their bulwark, that have before gored the gentle bosom of peace with pillage and robbery. Now, if these men have defeated the law and outrun native punishment, though they can outstrip men, they have no wings to fly from God: war is his beadle, war is his vengeance; so that here men are punish'd for before-breach of the king's laws in now the king's quarrel: where they fear'd the death, they have borne life away; and where they would be safe, they perish: then if they die unprovided, no more is the king guilty of their damnation, than he was before guilty of those impieties for the which they are now visited. Every subject's duty is the king's; but every subject's soul is his own. Therefore should every soldier in the wars do as every sick man in his bed, — wash every mote out of his conscience and dying so, death is to him advantage; or not dying, the time was blessedly lost wherein such preparation was gain'd: and in him that escapes, it were not sin to think that, making God so free an offer, He let him outlive that day to see His greatness, and to teach others how they should prepare.

MICHAEL WILLIAMS

'Tis certain, every man that dies ill, the ill upon his own head, — the king is not to answer it.

JOHN BATES

I do not desire he should answer for me; and yet I determine to fight lustily for him.

KING HENRY

I myself heard the king say he would not be ransom'd.

MICHAEL WILLIAMS

Ay, he said so, to make us fight cheerfully: but when our throats are cut, he may be ransom'd, and we ne'er the wiser.

KING HENRY

If I live to see it, I will never trust his word after.

MICHAEL WILLIAMS

'Mass, you'll pay him then! That's a perilous shot out of an elder-gun, that a poor and private displeasure can do against a monarch! you may as well go about to turn the sun to ice with fanning in his face with a peacock's feather. You'll never trust his word after! come, 'tis a foolish saying.

KING HENRY

Your reproof is something too round: I should be angry with you, if the time were convenient.

MICHAEL WILLIAMS

Let it be a quarrel between us, if you live.

KING HENRY

I embrace it.

MICHAEL WILLIAMS

How shall I know thee again?

KING HENRY

Give me any gage of thine, and I will wear it in my bonnet: then, if ever thou darest acknowledge it, I will make it my quarrel.

MICHAEL WILLIAMS

Here's my glove: give me another of thine.

KING HENRY

There.

MICHAEL WILLIAMS

This will I also wear in my cap: if ever thou come to me and say, after to-morrow, 'This is my glove,' by this hand, I will take thee a box on the ear.

KING HENRY

If ever I live to see it, I will challenge it.

MICHAEL WILLIAMS

Thou darest as well be hang'd.

KING HENRY

Well, I will do it, though I take thee in the king's company.

MICHAEL WILLIAMS

Keep thy word: fare thee well.

JOHN BATES

Be friends, you English fools, be friends: we have
French quarrels enow, if you could tell how to reckon.

KING HENRY

Indeed, the French may lay twenty French crowns to
one, they will beat us; for they bear them on their
shoulders: but it is no English treason to cut French
crowns; and to-morrow the king himself will be a
clipper.   [*Exeunt* SOLDIERS.
Upon the king! — let us our lives, our souls,
Our debts, our careful wives,
Our children, and our sins, lay on the king!
We must bear all. O hard condition,
Twin-born with greatness, subject to the breath
Of every fool, whose sense no more can feel
But his own wringing!
What infinite heart's-ease must kings neglect,
That private men enjoy!
And what have kings, that privates have not too,
Save ceremony, — save general ceremony?
And what art thou, thou idol ceremony?
What kind of god art thou, that suffer'st more
Of mortal griefs than do thy worshippers?
What are thy rents? what are thy comings-in?
O ceremony, show me but thy worth!
What is thy soul, O adoration?
Art thou aught else but place, degree, and form,
Creating awe and fear in other men?
Wherein thou art less happy being fear'd

74

Than they in fearing.
What drink'st thou oft, instead of homage sweet,
But poison'd flattery? O, be sick, great greatness,
And bid thy ceremony give thee cure!
Think'st thou the fiery fever will go out
With titles blown from adulation?
Will it give place to flexure and low bending?
Canst thou, when thou command'st the beggar's knee,
Command the health of it? No, thou proud dream,
That play'st so subtly with a king's repose:
I am a king that find thee; and I know
'Tis not the balm, the sceptre, and the ball,
The sword, the mace, the crown imperial,
The intertissued robe of gold and pearl,
The farced title running 'fore the king,
The throne he sits on, nor the tide of pomp
That beats upon the high shore of this world, —
No, not all these, thrice-gorgeous ceremony,
Not all these, laid in bed majestical,
Can sleep so soundly as the wretched slave,
Who, with a body fill'd and vacant mind,
Gets him to rest, cramm'd with distressful bread;
Never sees horrid night, the child of hell;
But, like a lackey, from the rise to set,
Sweats in the eye of Phœbus and all night
Sleeps in Elysium; next day, after dawn,
Doth rise, and help Hyperion to his horse;
And follows so the ever-running year,
With profitable labour, to his grave:
And, but for ceremony, such a wretch,
Winding up days with toil and nights with sleep,
Had the fore-hand and vantage of a king.
The slave, a member of the country's peace,
Enjoys it; but in gross brain little wots
What watch the king keeps to maintain the peace,
Whose hours the peasant best advantages.

Enter ERPINGHAM.

75

ERPINGHAM

My lord, your nobles, jealous of your absence,
Seek through your camp to find you.

KING HENRY

                           Good old knight,

Collect them all together at my tent:
I'll be before thee.

ERPINGHAM

              I shall do't, my lord.   *[Exit.*

KING HENRY

O God of battles! steel my soldiers' hearts;
Possess them not with fear; take from them now
The sense of reckoning, if th'opposed numbers
Pluck their hearts from them! — Not to-day, O Lord,
O, not to-day, think not upon the fault
My father made in compassing the crown!
I Richard's body have interred new;
And on it have bestow'd more contrite tears
Than from it issued forced drops of blood:
Five hundred poor I have in yearly pay,
Who twice a-day their wither'd hands hold up
Toward heaven, to pardon blood; and I have built
Two chantries, where the sad and solemn priests
Sing still for Richard's soul. More will I do;
Though all that I can do is nothing worth,
Since that my penitence comes after all,
Imploring pardon.

                 Enter GLOSTER.

GLOSTER

My liege!

KING HENRY

         My brother Gloster's voice? — Ay;
I know thy errand, I will go with thee: —
The day, my friends, and all things stay for me.   *[Exeunt.*

SCENE II

The French camp.

Enter the DAUPHIN, ORLEANS,
RAMBURES, *and others.*

ORLEANS
The sun doth gild our armour; up, my lords!

DAUPHIN
Montez à cheval! — My horse! *varlet, laquais!* ha!

ORLEANS
O brave spirit!

DAUPHIN
Via! — *les eaux et la terre,* —

ORLEANS
Rien puis? l'air et le feu, —

DAUPHIN
Ciel! cousin Orleans.

Enter CONSTABLE.

Now, my lord Constable!

CONSTABLE
Hark, how our steeds for present service neigh!

DAUPHIN
Mount them, and make incision in their hides,
That their hot blood may spin in English eyes,
And dout them with superfluous courage, ha!

RAMBURES
What, will you have them weep our horses' blood?
How shall we, then, behold their natural tears?

Enter a MESSENGER.

MESSENGER
The English are embattled, you French peers.

CONSTABLE
To horse, you gallant princes! straight to horse!
Do but behold yond poor and starved band,
And your fair show shall suck away their souls,
Leaving them but the shales and husks of men.

There is not work enough for all our hands;
Scarce blood enough in all their sickly veins
To give each naked curtle-axe a stain,
That our French gallants shall to-day draw out,
And sheathe for lack of sport: let us but blow on them,
The vapour of our valour will o'erturn them.
'Tis positive 'gainst all exceptions, lords,
That our superfluous lackeys and our peasants, —
Who in unnecessary action swarm
About our squares of battle, — were enow
To purge this field of such a hilding foe;
Though we upon this mountain's basis by
Took stand for idle speculation, —
But that our honours must not. What's to say?
A very little little let us do,
And all is done. Then let the trumpets sound
The tucket-sonance and the note to mount:
For our approach shall so much dare the field,
That England shall couch down in fear, and yield.

Enter GRANDPRÉ.

GRANDPRÉ
Why do you stay so long, my lords of France?
Yond island carrions, desperate of their bones,
Ill-favouredly become the morning field:
Their ragged curtains poorly are let loose,
And our air shakes them passing scornfully:
Big Mars seems bankrout in their beggar'd host,
And faintly through a rusty beaver peeps:
The horsemen sit like fixed candlesticks,
With torch-staves in their hand; and their poor jades
Lob down their heads, dropping the hides and hips,
The gum down-roping from their pale-dead eyes,
And in their pale dull mouths the gimmal-bit
Lies foul with chew'd grass, still and motionless;
And their executors, the knavish crows,
Fly o'er them, all impatient for their hour.
Description cannot suit itself in words

To demonstrate the life of such a battle
In life so lifeless as it shows itself.

CONSTABLE

They have said their prayers, and they stay for death.

DAUPHIN

Shall we go send them dinners and fresh suits,
And give their fasting horses provender,
And after fight with them?

CONSTABLE

I stay but for my guidon: — to the field! —
I will the banner from a trumpet take,
And use it for my haste. Come, come, away!
The sun is high, and we outwear the day.

[*Exeunt.*

SCENE III

The English camp.

Enter GLOSTER, BEDFORD, EXETER,
ERPINGHAM, *with all his host;* SALISBURY, *and*
WESTMORELAND.

GLOSTER

Where is the king?

BEDFORD

The king himself is rode to view the battle.

WESTMORELAND

Of fighting-men they have full three-score thousand.

EXETER

There's five to one; besides, they all are fresh.

SALISBURY

God's arm strike with us! 'tis a fearful odds.
God b' wi' you, princes all; I'll to my charge:
If we no more meet till we meet in heaven,
Then, joyfully, — my noble Lord of Bedford, —
My dear Lord Gloster, — and my good Lord Exeter, —
And my kind kinsman, — warriors all, adieu!

BEDFORD

Farewell, good Salisbury; and good luck go with thee!

EXETER

Farewell, kind lord; fight valiantly to-day:
And yet I do thee wrong to mind thee of it,
For thou art fram'd of the firm truth of valour.

[*Exit* SALISBURY.

BEDFORD

He is as full of valour as of kindness;
Princely in both.

Enter KING HENRY.

WESTMORELAND

O, that we now had here
But one ten thousand of those men in England
That do no work to-day!

KING HENRY

What's he that wishes so?
My cousin Westmoreland? — No, my fair cousin:
If we are mark'd to die, we are enow
To do our country loss; and if to live,
The fewer men, the greater share of honour.
God's will! I pray thee, wish not one man more.
By Jove, I am not covetous for gold;
Nor care I who doth feed upon my cost;
It yearns me not if men my garments wear;
Such outward things dwell not in my desires:
But if it be a sin to covet honour,
I am the most offending soul alive.
No, faith, my coz, wish not a man from England:
God's peace! I would not lose so great an honour,
As one man more, methinks, would share from me,
For the best hope I have. O, do not wish one more!
Rather proclaim it, Westmoreland, through my host,
That he which hath no stomach to this fight,
Let him depart; his passport shall be made,
And crowns for convoy put into his purse:
We would not die in that man's company

That fears his fellowship to die with us.
This day is call'd the feast of Crispian:
He that outlives this day, and comes safe home,
Will stand a tip-toe when the day is named,
And rouse him at the name of Crispian.
He that shall live this day, and see old age,
Will yearly on the vigil feast his neighbours,
And say, 'To-morrow is Saint Crispian':
Then will he strip his sleeve and show his scars,
And say, 'These wounds I had on Crispin's day.'
Old men forget: yet all shall be forgot,
But he'll remember with advantages
What feats he did that day: then shall our names,
Familiar in their mouths as household words, —
Harry the king, Bedford and Exeter,
Warwick and Talbot, Salisbury and Gloster, —
Be in their flowing cups freshly remember'd.
This story shall the good man teach his son;
And Crispin Crispian shall ne'er go by,
From this day to the ending of the world,
But we in it shall be remembered, —
We few, we happy few, we band of brothers;
For he to-day that sheds his blood with me
Shall be my brother; be he ne'er so vile,
This day shall gentle his condition:
And gentlemen in England now a-bed
Shall think themselves accurs't they were not here;
And hold their manhoods cheap whiles any speaks
That fought with us upon Saint Crispin's day.

Enter SALISBURY.

SALISBURY

My sovereign lord, bestow yourself with speed:
The French are bravely in their battles set,
And will with all expedience charge on us.

KING HENRY

All things are ready, if our minds be so.

WESTMORELAND

Perish the man whose mind is backward now!

KING HENRY

Thou dost not wish more help from England, coz?

WESTMORELAND

God's will! my liege, would you and I alone,
Without more help, could fight this royal battle out!

KING HENRY

Why, now thou hast unwish'd five thousand men;
Which likes me better than to wish us one. —
You know your places: God be with you all!

Tucket. Enter MONTJOY.

MONTJOY

Once more I come to know of thee, King Harry,
If for thy ransom thou wilt now compound,
Before thy most assured overthrow:
For certainly thou art so near the gulf,
Thou needs must be englutted. Besides, in mercy,
The Constable desires thee thou wilt mind
Thy followers of repentance; that their souls
May make a peaceful and a sweet retire
From off these fields, where, wretches, their poor bodies
Must lie and fester.

KING HENRY

　　　　　　Who hath sent thee now?

MONTJOY

The Constable of France.

KING HENRY

I pray thee, bear my former answer back:
Bid them achieve me, and then sell my bones.
Good God! why should they mock poor fellows thus?
The man that once did sell the lion's skin
While the beast liv'd, was kill'd with hunting him.
A many of our bodies shall no doubt
Find native graves; upon the which, I trust,
Shall witness live in brass of this day's work:
And those that leave their valiant bones in France,

Dying like men, though buried in your dunghills,
They shall be fam'd; for there the sun shall greet them,
And draw their honours reeking up to heaven;
Leaving their earthly parts to choke your clime,
The smell whereof shall breed a plague in France.
Mark, then, abounding valour in our English;
That, being dead, like to the bullet's grazing,
Break out into a second course of mischief,
Killing in relapse of mortality.
Let me speak proudly: — tell the Constable
We are but warriors for the working-day;
Our gayness and our gilt are all besmirch'd
With rainy marching in the painful field;
There's not a piece of feather in our host, —
Good argument, I hope, we will not fly, —
And time hath worn us into slovenry:
But, by the mass, our hearts are in the trim;
And my poor soldiers tell me, yet ere night
They'll be in fresher robes; or they will pluck
The gay new coats o'er the French soldiers' heads,
And turn them out of service. If they do this, —
As, if God please, they shall, — my ransom then
Will soon be levied. Herald, save thou thy labour;
Come thou no more for ransom, gentle herald:
They shall have none, I swear, but these my joints, —
Which if they have as I will leave 'em them,
Shall yield them little, tell the Constable.

MONTJOY

I shall, King Harry. And so, fare thee well:
Thou never shalt hear herald any more.   [*Exit.*

KING HENRY

I fear thou'lt once more come again for ransom.

Enter YORK.

YORK

My lord, most humbly on my knee I beg
The leading of the vaward.

KING HENRY

Take it, brave York. — Now, soldiers, march away: —
And how thou pleasest, God, dispose the day!   [*Exeunt.*

SCENE IV

The field of battle.

Alarum: excursions. Enter PISTOL, French SOLDIER,
and BOY.

PISTOL

Yield, cur!

FRENCH SOLDIER

Je pense que vous êtes le gentilhomme de bonne qualité.

PISTOL

Qualitie calmie custure me! Art thou a gentleman? what is
thy name? discuss.

FRENCH SOLDIER

O Seigneur Dieu!

PISTOL

O, Signieur Dew should be a gentleman: —
Perpend my words, O Signieur Dew, and mark; —
O Signieur Dew, thou diest on point of fox,
Except, O Signieur, thou do give to me
Egregious ransom.

FRENCH SOLDIER

O, prenez miséricorde! ayez pitié de moy!

PISTOL

Moy shall not serve; I will have forty moys;
Or I will fetch thy rim out at thy throat
In drops of crimson blood.

FRENCH SOLDIER

Est-il impossible d'échapper la force de ton bras?

PISTOL

Brass, cur!
Thou damned and luxurious mountain-goat,
Offer'st me brass?

PISTOL Bid him prepare, for I will cut his throat.

FRENCH SOLDIER

  O, pardonnez-moy!

PISTOL

  Say'st thou me so? is that a ton of moys? —
  Come hither, boy: ask me this slave in French
  What is his name.

BOY

  Écoutez: comment êtes-vous appelé?

FRENCH SOLDIER

  Monsieur le Fer.

BOY

  He says his name is Master Fer.

PISTOL

  Master Fer! I'll fer him, and firk him, and ferret him: —
  discuss the same in French unto him.

BOY

  I do not know the French for fer, and ferret, and firk.

PISTOL

  Bid him prepare; for I will cut his throat.

FRENCH SOLDIER

  Que dit-il, monsieur?

BOY

Il me commande de vous dire que vous faites vous prêt; car ce soldat ici est disposé tout à cette heure de couper votre gorge.

PISTOL

Owy, cuppele gorge, permafoy,
Peasant, unless thou give me crowns, brave crowns;
Or mangled shalt thou be by this my sword.

FRENCH SOLDIER

O, je vous supplie, pour l'amour de Dieu, me pardonner! Je suis gentilhomme de bonne maison: gardez ma vie, et je vous donnerai deux cents écus.

PISTOL

What are his words?

BOY

He prays you to save his life: he is a gentleman of a good house; and for his ransom he will give you two hundred crowns.

PISTOL

Tell him my fury shall abate, and I
The crowns will take.

FRENCH SOLDIER

Petit monsieur, que dit-il?

BOY

Encore qu'il est contre son jurement de pardonner aucun prisonnier, néanmoins, pour les écus que vous l'avez promis, il est content de vous donner la liberté, le franchisement.

FRENCH SOLDIER

Sur mes genoux je vous donne mille remercîmens; et je m'estime heureux que je suis tombé entre les mains d'un chevalier, je pense, le plus brave, vaillant, et très distingué seigneur d'Angleterre.

PISTOL

Expound unto me, boy.

BOY

He gives you, upon his knees, a thousand thanks; and he esteems himself happy that he hath fall'n into the hands

of one, as he thinks, the most brave, valorous, and
thrice-worthy signieur of England.

PISTOL

As I suck blood, I will some mercy show. — Follow me,
cur.   [*Exit.*

BOY

Suivez-vous le grand capitaine. [*Exit* FRENCH
SOLDIER.] I did never know so full a voice issue from
so empty a heart: but the saying is true, — The empty
vessel makes the greatest sound. Bardolph and Nym had
ten times more valour than this roaring devil i'th'old
play, that every one may pare his nails with a wooden
dagger; and they are both hang'd; and so would this be,
if he durst steal any thing adventurously. I must stay
with the lackeys, with the luggage of our camp: the
French might have a good prey of us, if he knew of it;
for there is none to guard it but boys.   [*Exit.*

SCENE V

Another part of the field.
Enter CONSTABLE, ORLEANS, BOURBON,
 DAUPHIN, RAMBURES, and others.

CONSTABLE

O diable!

ORLEANS

O Seigneur! — le jour est perdu, tout est perdu!

DAUPHIN

Mort de ma vie! all is confounded, all!
Reproach and everlasting shame
Sits mocking in our plumes. — *O méchante fortune!* —
Do not run away.   [*A short alarum.*

CONSTABLE

          Why, all our ranks are broke.

DAUPHIN

O perdurable shame! — let's stab ourselves.

87

Be these the wretches that we play'd at dice for?

ORLEANS

Is this the king we sent to for his ransom?

BOURBON

Shame, and eternal shame, nothing but shame!
Let's die in honour: once more back again;
And he that will not follow Bourbon now,
Let him go hence, and with his cap in hand,
Like a base pandar, hold the chamber-door
Whilst by a slave, no gentler than my dog,
His fairest daughter is contaminate.

CONSTABLE

Disorder, that hath spoil'd us, friend us now!
Let us on heaps go offer up our lives.

ORLEANS

We are enow, yet living in the field,
To smother up the English in our throngs,
If any order might be thought upon.

BOURBON

The devil take order now! I'll to the throng:
Let life be short; else shame will be too long.   [*Exeunt.*

SCENE VI

Another part of the field.

Alarum. Enter KING HENRY and FORCES,
   EXETER, and others.

KING HENRY

Well have we done, thrice-valiant countrymen:
But all's not done; yet keep the French the field.

EXETER

The Duke of York commends him to your majesty.

KING HENRY

Lives he, good uncle? thrice within this hour
I saw him down; thrice up again, and fighting;
From helmet to the spur all blood he was.

EXETER

In which array, brave soldier, doth he lie,
Larding the plain; and by his bloody side,
Yoke-fellow to his honour-owing wounds,
The noble Earl of Suffolk also lies.
Suffolk first died: and York, all haggled over,
Comes to him, where in gore he lay insteep'd,
And takes him by the beard; kisses the gashes
That bloodily did yawn upon his face;
And cries aloud, 'Tarry, dear cousin Suffolk!
My soul shall thine keep company to heaven;
Tarry, sweet soul, for mine; then fly abreast;
As in this glorious and well-foughten field
We kept together in our chivalry!'
Upon these words I came, and cheer'd him up:
He smil'd me in the face, raught me his hand,
And, with a feeble gripe, says, 'Dear my lord,
Commend my service to my sovereign.'
So did he turn, and over Suffolk's neck
He threw his wounded arm, and kiss'd his lips;
And so, espous'd to death, with blood he seal'd
A testament of noble-ending love.
The pretty and sweet manner of it forc'd
Those waters from me which I would have stopp'd;
But I had not so much of man in me,
And all my mother came into mine eyes,
And gave me up to tears.

KING HENRY

       I blame you not;
For, hearing this, I must perforce compound
With mistful eyes, or they will issue too. — [*Alarum.*
But, hark! what new alarum is this same? —
The French have reinforc'd their scatter'd men: —
Then every soldier kill his prisoners;
Give the word through.   [*Exeunt.*

SCENE VII

Another part of the field.

Enter FLUELLEN and GOWER.

FLUELLEN

Kill the poys and the luggage! 'tis expressly against the
law of arms: 'tis as arrant a piece of knavery, mark you
now, as can be offer't; in your conscience, now, is it not?

GOWER

'Tis certain there's not a boy left alive; and the cowardly
rascals that ran from the battle ha' done this slaughter:
besides, they have burn'd and carried away all that was
in the king's tent; wherefore the king, most worthily,
hath caused every soldier to cut his prisoner's throat. O,
'tis a gallant king!

FLUELLEN

Ay, he was porn at Monmouth, Captain Gower. What call
you the town's name where Alexander the Pig was porn!

GOWER

Alexander the Great.

FLUELLEN

Why, I pray you, is not pig great? the pig, or the great,
or the mighty, or the huge, or the magnanimous, are all
one reckonings, save the phrase is a little variations.

GOWER

I think Alexander the Great was born in Macedon: his
father was call'd Philip of Macedon, as I take it.

FLUELLEN

I think it is in Macedon where Alexander is porn. I tell
you, captain, if you look in the maps of the 'orld, I
warrant you sall find, in the comparisons between
Macedon and Monmouth, that the situations, look you,
is both alike. There is a river in Macedon; and there is
also moreover a river at Monmouth: it is called Wye at
Monmouth; but it is out of my prains what is the name
of the other river; but 'tis all one, 'tis alike as my fingers
is to my fingers, and there is salmons in both. If you

mark Alexander's life well, Harry of Monmouth's life is
come after it indifferent well; for there is figures in all
things. Alexander, — Got knows, and you know, — in
his rages, and his furies, and his wraths, and his cholers,
and his moods, and his displeasures, and his
indignations, and also being a little intoxicates in his
prains, did, in his ales and his angers, look you, kill his
pest friend, Cleitus.

GOWER

Our king is not like him in that: he never kill'd any of his
friends.

FLUELLEN

It is not well done, mark you now, take the tales out of
my mouth, ere it is made and finish't. I speak but in the
figures and comparisons of it: as Alexander kill'd his
friend Cleitus, being in his ales and his cups; so also
Harry Monmouth, being in his right wits and his goot
judgements, turn'd away the fat knight with the great-
pelly doublet: he was full of jests, and gipes, and
knaveries, and mocks; I have forgot his name.

GOWER

Sir John Falstaff.

FLUELLEN

That is he: — I'll tell you there is goot men porn at
Monmouth.

GOWER

Here comes his majesty.

Alarum. Enter KING HENRY, *and* FORCES;
WARWICK, GLOSTER, EXETER, *and others.*

KING HENRY

I was not angry since I came to France
Until this instant. — Take a trumpet, herald;
Ride thou unto the horsemen on yond hill:
If they will fight with us, bid them come down,
Or void the field; they do offend our sight:
If they'll do neither, we will come to them,
And make them skirr away, as swift as stones

Enforced from the old Assyrian slings:
Besides, we'll cut the throats of those we have;
And not a man of them that we shall take
Shall taste our mercy: — go, and tell them so.

EXETER

Here comes the herald of the French, my liege.

GLOSTER

His eyes are humbler than they us'd to be.

Enter MONTJOY.

KING HENRY

How now! what means this, herald? know'st thou not
That I have fin'd these bones of mine for ransom?
Comest thou again for ransom?

MONTJOY

               No, great king:
I come to thee for charitable licence
That we may wander o'er this bloody field
To look our dead, and then to bury them;
To sort our nobles from our common men;
For many of our princes — woe the while —
Lie drown'd and soak'd in mercenary blood;
So do our vulgar drench their peasant limbs
In blood of princes; and their wounded steeds
Fret fetlock deep in gore, and with wild rage
Yerk out their armed heels at their dead masters,
Killing them twice. O, give us leave, great king,
To view the field in safety, and dispose
Of their dead bodies!

KING HENRY

            I tell thee truly, herald,
I know not if the day be ours or no;
For yet a many of your horsemen peer
And gallop o'er the field.

MONTJOY

            The day is yours.

KING HENRY

Praised be God, and not our strength, for it! —

What is this castle call'd that stands hard by?

MONTJOY

They call it Agincourt.

KING HENRY

Then call we this the field of Agincourt,
Fought on the day of Crispin Crispianus.

FLUELLEN

Your grandfather of famous memory, an't please your
majesty, and your great-uncle Edward the Plack Prince
of Wales, as I have read in the chronicles, fought a most
prave pattle here in France.

KING HENRY

They did, Fluellen.

FLUELLEN

Your majesty says very true: if your majesties is
remember'd of it, the Welshmen did goot service in a
garden where leeks did grow, wearing leeks in their
Monmouth caps; which, your majesty knows, to this
hour is an honourable padge of the service; and I do
pelieve your majesty takes no scorn to wear the leek
upon Saint Tavy's day.

KING HENRY

I wear it for a memorable honour;
For I am Welsh, you know, good countryman.

FLUELLEN

All the water in Wye cannot wash your majesty's Welsh
plood out of your pody, I can tell you that: God pless it,
and preserve it, as long as it pleases his Grace, and his
majesty too!

KING HENRY

Thanks, good my countryman.

FLUELLEN

By Cheshu, I am your majesty's countryman, I care not
who know it; I will confess it to all the 'orld: I need not
to be ashamed of your majesty, praised be Got, so long
as your majesty is an honest man.

KING HENRY

God keep me so! — Our heralds go with him:
Bring me just notice of the numbers dead
On both our parts. — Call yonder fellow hither.

[*Points to* WILLIAMS.
Exeunt HERALDS *with* MONTJOY.

EXETER

Soldier, you must come to the king.

KING HENRY

Soldier, why wear'st thou that glove in thy cap?

MICHAEL WILLIAMS

An't please your majesty, 'tis the gage of one that
I should fight withal, if he be alive.

KING HENRY

An Englishman?

MICHAEL WILLIAMS

An't please your majesty, a rascal that swagger'd with
me last night; who, if alive, and ever dare to challenge
this glove, I have sworn to take him a box o'th'ear: or if
I can see my glove in his cap, which he swore, as he was
a soldier, he would wear if alive, I will strike it out
soundly.

KING HENRY

What think you, Captain Fluellen? is it fit this soldier
keep his oath?

FLUELLEN

He is a craven and a villain else, an't please your
majesty, in my conscience.

KING HENRY

It may be his enemy is a gentleman of great sort, quite
from the answer of his degree.

FLUELLEN

Though he be as goot a gentleman as the tevil is, as
Lucifer and Belzebub himself, it is necessary, look your
Grace, that he keep his vow and his oath: if he be
perjured, see you now, his reputation is as arrant a

villain and a Jack-sauce, as ever his plack shoe trod upon
Got's ground and his earth, in my conscience, la.

KING HENRY

Then keep thy vow, sirrah, when thou meet'st the
fellow.

MICHAEL WILLIAMS

So I will, my liege, as I live.

KING HENRY

Who servest thou under?

MICHAEL WILLIAMS

Under Captain Gower, my liege.

FLUELLEN

Gower is a goot captain, and is good knowledge and
literatured in the wars.

KING HENRY

Call him hither to me, soldier.

MICHAEL WILLIAMS

I will, my liege.   [*Exit.*

KING HENRY

Here, Fluellen; wear thou this favour for me, and stick it
in thy cap: when Alençon and myself were down
together, I pluck'd this glove from his helm: if any man
challenge this, he is a friend to Alençon, and an enemy
to our person; if thou encounter any such, apprehend
him, an thou dost me love.

FLUELLEN

Your Grace does me as great honours as can be desired
in the hearts of his subjects: I would fain see the man,
that has but two legs, that shall find himself aggriefed at
this glove; that is all; but I would fain see it once, an
please Got of his grace that I might see.

KING HENRY

Know'st thou Gower?

FLUELLEN

He is my dear friend, an please you.

KING HENRY
Pray thee, go seek him, and bring him to my tent.

FLUELLEN
I will fetch him.

KING HENRY
My Lord of Warwick, and my brother Gloster,
Follow Fluellen closely at the heels:
The glove which I have given him for a favour
May haply purchase him a box o'th'ear;
It is the soldier's; I, by bargain, should
Wear it myself. Follow, good cousin Warwick:
If that the soldier strike him, — as I judge
By his blunt bearing, he will keep his word, —
Some sudden mischief may arise of it;
For I do know Fluellen valiant,
And, touch'd with choler, hot as gunpowder,
And quickly will return an injury:
Follow, and see there be no harm between them. —
Go you with me, uncle of Exeter.   [*Exeunt.*

SCENE VIII

Before KING HENRY'S *pavilion.*
Enter GOWER and WILLIAMS.

MICHAEL WILLIAMS
I warrant it is to knight you, captain.

Enter FLUELLEN.

FLUELLEN
God's will and his pleasure, captain, I peseech you now,
come apace to the king: there is more goot toward you
peradventure than is in your knowledge to dream of.

MICHAEL WILLIAMS
Sir, know you this glove?

FLUELLEN
Know the glove! I know the glove is a glove.

96

MICHAEL WILLIAMS

I know this; and thus I challenge it.   [*Strikes him.*

FLUELLEN

'Splood, an arrant traitor as any's in the universal 'orld,
or in France, or in England!

GOWER

How now, sir! you villain!

MICHAEL WILLIAMS

Do you think I'll be forsworn?

FLUELLEN

Stand away, Captain Gower; I will give treason his
payment into plows, I warrant you.

MICHAEL WILLIAMS

I am no traitor.

FLUELLEN

That's a lie in thy throat. — I charge you in his
majesty's name, apprehend him: he's a friend of the
Duke Alençon's.

    Enter WARWICK *and* GLOSTER.

WARWICK

How now, how now! what's the matter?

FLUELLEN

My Lord of Warwick, here is — praised be Got for it! —
a most contagious treason come to light, look you, as you
shall desire in a summer's day. — Here is his majesty.

    Enter KING HENRY *and* EXETER.

KING HENRY

How now! what's the matter?

FLUELLEN

My liege, here is a villain and a traitor, that, look your
Grace, has struck the glove which your majesty is take
out of the helmet of Alençon.

MICHAEL WILLIAMS

My liege, this was my glove; here is the fellow of it; and he
that I gave it to in change promised to wear it in his cap: I

promised to strike him, if he did: I met this man with my
glove in his cap, and I have been as good as my word.

FLUELLEN

Your majesty hear now, saving your majesty's manhood,
what an arrant, rascally, beggarly, lousy knave it is: I
hope your majesty is pear me testimony, and witness,
and will avouchment, that this is the glove of Alençon,
that your majesty is give me, in your conscience, now.

KING HENRY

Give me thy glove, soldier: look, here is the fellow of it.
'Twas I, indeed, thou promised'st to strike;
And thou hast given me most bitter terms.

FLUELLEN

An please your majesty, let his neck answer for it, if
there is any martial law in the 'orld.

KING HENRY

How canst thou make me satisfaction?

MICHAEL WILLIAMS

All offences, my liege, come from the heart: never came
any from mine that might offend your majesty.

KING HENRY

It was ourself thou didst abuse.

MICHAEL WILLIAMS

Your majesty came not like yourself: you appear'd to me
but as a common man; witness the night, your
garments, your lowliness; and what your highness
suffer'd under that shape, I beseech you take it for your
own fault, and not mine: for had you been as I took you
for, I made no offence; therefore, I beseech your
highness, pardon me.

KING HENRY

Here, uncle Exeter, fill this glove with crowns,
And give it to this fellow. — Keep it, fellow;
And wear it for an honour in thy cap
Till I do challenge it. — Give him the crowns: —
And, captain, you must needs be friends with him.

FLUELLEN

By this day and this light, the fellow has mettle enough
in his pelly. — Hold, there is twelve pence for you; and I
pray you to serve Got, and keep you out of prawls, and
prabbles, and quarrels, and dissensions, and, I warrant
you, it is the better for you.

MICHAEL WILLIAMS

I will none of your money.

FLUELLEN

It is with a goot will; I can tell you, it will serve you to
mend your shoes: come, wherefore should you be so
pashful? your shoes is not so goot; 'tis a good silling, I
warrant you, or I will change it.

Enter an English HERALD.

KING HENRY

Now, herald, — are the dead number'd?

HERALD

Here is the number of the slaughter'd French.

[*Delivers a paper.*

KING HENRY

What prisoners of good sort are taken, uncle?

EXETER

Charles Duke of Orleans, nephew to the king;
John Duke of Bourbon, and Lord Bouciqualt:
Of other lords and barons, knights and squires,
Full fifteen hundred, besides common men.

KING HENRY

This note doth tell me of ten thousand French
That in the field lie slain: of princes, in this number,
And nobles bearing banners, there lie dead
One hundred twenty-six: added to these,
Of knights, esquires, and gallant gentlemen,
Eight thousand and four hundred; of the which,
Five hundred were but yesterday dubb'd knights:
So that, in these ten thousand they have lost,
There are but sixteen hundred mercenaries;

The rest are princes, barons, lords, knights, squires,
And gentlemen of blood and quality.
The names of those their nobles that lie dead, —
Charles Delabreth, high-Constable of France;
Jaques of Chatillon, admiral of France;
The master of the cross-bows, Lord Rambures;
Great-master of France, the brave Sir Guiscard
    Dauphin;
John Duke of Alençon; Antony Duke of Brabant,
The brother of the Duke of Burgundy;
And Edward Duke of Bar: of lusty earls,
Grandpré and Roussi, Fauconberg and Foix,
Beaumont and Marle, Vaudemont and Lestrale.
Here was a royal fellowship of death! —
Where is the number of our English dead? —
            [HERALD *presents another paper.*
Edward the Duke of York, the Earl of Suffolk,
Sir Richard Ketly, Davy Gam, esquire;
None else of name; and of all other men
But five and twenty. — O God, Thy arm was here;
And not to us, but to Thy arm alone,
Ascribe we all! — When, without stratagem,
But in plain shock and even play of battle,
Was ever known so great and little loss
On one part and on th'other? — Take it, God,
For it is only thine!

EXETER

         'Tis wonderful!

KING HENRY

Come, go we in procession to the village:
And be it death proclaimed through our host
To boast of this, or take the praise from God
Which is His only.

FLUELLEN

Is it not lawful, an please your majesty, to tell how many
is kill'd?

KING HENRY

Yes, captain; but with this acknowledgement,
That God fought for us.

FLUELLEN

Yes, my conscience, He did us great goot.

KING HENRY

Do we all holy rites:
Let there be sung *Non nobis* and *Te Deum*.
The dead with charity enclos'd in clay,
We'll then to Calais; and to England then;
Where ne'er from France arriv'd more happy men.

[*Exeunt.*

ACT V

PROLOGUE

Enter CHORUS.

CHORUS

Vouchsafe to those that have not read the story,
That I may prompt them: and of such as have,
I humbly pray them to admit th'excuse
Of time, of numbers, and due course of things,
Which cannot in their huge and proper life
Be here presented. Now we bear the king
Toward Calais: grant him there; there seen,
Heave him away upon your winged thoughts
Athwart the sea. Behold, the English beach
Pales in the flood with men, with wives, and boys,
Whose shouts and claps out-voice the deep-mouth'd
    sea,
Which, like a mighty whiffler 'fore the king,
Seems to prepare his way: so let him land;
And solemnly see him set on to London.
So swift a pace hath thought, that even now
You may imagine him upon Blackheath;

Where that his lords desire him to have borne
His bruised helmet and his bended sword
Before him through the city: he forbids it,
Being free from vainness and self-glorious pride;
Giving full trophy, signal, and ostent,
Quite from himself to God. But now behold,
In the quick forge and working-house of thought,
How London doth pour out her citizens!
The mayor, and all his brethren, in best sort, —
Like to the senators of th'antique Rome,
With the plebeians swarming at their heels, —
Go forth, and fetch their conquering Cæsar in:
As, by a lower but loving likelihood,
Were now the general of our gracious empress —
As in good time he may — from Ireland coming,
Bringing rebellion broached on his sword,
How many would the peaceful city quit,
To welcome him! much more, and much more cause,
Did they this Harry. Now in London place him; —
As yet the lamentation of the French
Invites the King of England's stay at home; —
The emperor's coming in behalf of France,
To order peace between them; — and omit
All the occurrences, whatever chanc'd,
Till Harry's back-return again to France:
There must we bring him; and myself have play'd
The interim, by remembering you 'tis past.
Then brook abridgement; and your eyes advance,
After your thoughts, straight back again to France.

[*Exit.*

SCENE I

France. The English camp.
Enter FLUELLEN and GOWER.

GOWER

Nay, that's right; but why wear you your leek to-day?
Saint Davy's day is past.

FLUELLEN

There is occasions and causes why and wherefore in all
things: I will tell you, asse my friend, Captain Gower: —
the rascally, scald, peggarly, lousy, pragging knave,
Pistol, — which you and yourself, and all the 'orld,
know to be no petter than a fellow, look you now, of no
merits, — he is come to me, and prings me pread and
salt yesterday, look you, and pid me eat my leek: it was
in a place where I could not preed no contention with
him; but I will be so pold as to wear it in my cap till I
see him once again, and then I will tell him a little piece
of my desires.

GOWER

Why, here he comes, swelling like a turkeycock.

FLUELLEN

'Tis no matter for his swellings nor his turkeycocks.

Enter PISTOL.

God pless you, Auncient Pistol! you scurvy, lousy knave,
God pless you!

PISTOL

Ha! art thou bedlam? dost thou thirst, base Trojan,
To have me fold up Parca's fatal web?
Hence! I am qualmish at the smell of leek.

FLUELLEN

I peseech you heartily, scurvy, lousy knave, at my
desires, and my requests, and my petitions, to eat, look
you, this leek; because, look you, you do not love it, nor
your affections, and your appetites, and your digestions,
does not agree with it, I would desire you to eat it.

PISTOL

Not for Cadwallader and all his goats.

FLUELLEN

There is one goat for you. [*Strikes him.*] Will you be so goot, scald knave, as eat it?

PISTOL

Base Trojan, thou shalt die.

FLUELLEN

You say very true, scald knave, — when Got's will is: I will desire you to live in the mean time, and eat your victuals: come, there is sauce for it. [*Strikes him again.*] You call'd me yesterday mountain-squire; but I will make you to-day a squire of low degree. I pray you, fall to: if you can mock a leek, you can eat a leek.

GOWER

Enough, captain: you have astonish'd him.

FLUELLEN

I say, I will make him eat some part of my leek, or I will peat his pate four days. — Pite, I pray you; it is good for your green wound and your ploody coxcomb.

PISTOL

Must I bite?

FLUELLEN

Yes, certainly, and out of doubt, and out of question too, and ambiguities.

PISTOL

By this leek, I will most horribly revenge:
I eat and eat, I swear —

FLUELLEN

Eat, I pray you: will you have some more sauce to your leek? there is not enough leek to swear by.

PISTOL

Quiet thy cudgel; thou dost see I eat.

FLUELLEN

Much goot do you, scald knave, heartily. Nay, pray you, throw none away; the skin is goot for your proken coxcomb. When you take occasions to see leeks hereafter, I pray you, mock at 'em; that is all.

FLUELLEN I pray you, fall to: if you can mock a leek, you can eat a leek.

PISTOL
  Good.

FLUELLEN
  Ay, leeks is goot: — hold you, there is a groat to heal
  your pate.

PISTOL
  Me a groat!

FLUELLEN
  Yes, verily and in truth, you shall take it; or I have
  another leek in my pocket, which you shall eat.

PISTOL
  I take thy groat in earnest of revenge.

FLUELLEN
  If I owe you any thing, I will pay you in cudgels; you shall
  be a woodmonger, and buy nothing of me but cudgels.
  Got b' wi' you, and keep you, and heal your pate.   [*Exit.*

PISTOL
  All hell shall stir for this.

GOWER

Go, go; you are a counterfeit cowardly knave. Will you
mock at an ancient tradition, — begun upon an
honourable respect, and worn as a memorable trophy of
predeceased valour, — and dare not avouch in your
deeds any of your words? I have seen you gleeking and
galling at this gentleman twice or thrice. You thought,
because he could not speak English in the native garb,
he could not therefore handle an English cudgel: you
find it otherwise; and henceforth let a Welsh correction
teach you a good English condition. Fare ye well.   [*Exit.*

PISTOL

Doth Fortune play the huswife with me now?
News have I, that my Nell is dead i' the spital
Of malady of France;
And there my rendezvous is quite cut off.
Old I do wax; and from my weary limbs
Honour is cudgell'd. Well, bawd will I turn,
And something lean to cutpurse of quick hand.
To England will I steal, and there I'll steal:
And patches will I get unto these scars,
And swear I got them in the Gallia wars.   [*Exit.*

SCENE II

France. The French KING'S *palace.*

Enter, at one door, KING HENRY, BEDFORD,
GLOSTER, EXETER, WARWICK,
WESTMORELAND, *and other* LORDS; *at another, the*
French KING, QUEEN ISABEL, *the* PRINCESS
KATHARINE, ALICE, *other* LADIES, *and* LORDS; *the*
DUKE *of* BURGUNDY, *and his* TRAIN.

KING HENRY

Peace to this meeting, wherefore we are met!
Unto our brother France, and to our sister,
Health and fair time of day; — joy and good wishes
To our most fair and princely cousin Katharine; —

And, as a branch and member of this royalty,
By whom this great assembly is contrived,
We do salute you, Duke of Burgundy; —
And, princes French, and peers, health to you all!

FRENCH KING

Right joyous are we to behold your face,
Most worthy brother England; fairly met: —
So are you, princes English, every one.

FLUELLEN Right joyous are we to behold your face, most worthy
brother England.

QUEEN ISABEL

So happy be the issue, brother England,
Of this good day and of this gracious meeting,
As we are now glad to behold your eyes;
Your eyes, which hitherto have borne in them
Against the French, that met them in their bent,
The fatal balls of murdering basilisks:
The venom of such looks, we fairly hope,
Have lost their quality; and that this day
Shall change all griefs and quarrels into love.

KING HENRY

To cry amen to that, thus we appear.

QUEEN ISABEL

You English princes all, I do salute you.

BURGUNDY

My duty to you both, on equal love,
Great Kings of France and England! That I have
   labour'd,
With all my wits, my pains, and strong endeavours,
To bring your most imperial majesties
Unto this bar and royal interview,
Your mightiness on both parts best can witness.
Since, then, my office hath so far prevail'd,
That, face to face and royal eye to eye,
You have congreeted, let it not disgrace me,
If I demand, before this royal view,
What rub or what impediment there is,
Why that the naked, poor, and mangled Peace,
Dear nurse of arts, plenties, and joyful births,
Should not, in this best garden of the world,
Our fertile France, put up her lovely visage?
Alas, she hath from France too long been chased!
And all her husbandry doth lie on heaps,
Corrupting in its own fertility.
Her vine, the merry cheerer of the heart,
Unpruned dies; her hedges even-pleach'd,
Like prisoners wildly overgrown with hair,

Put forth disorder'd twigs; her fallow leas
The darnel, hemlock, and rank fumitory,
Do root upon, while that the coulter rusts,
That should deracinate such savagery;
The even mead, that erst brought sweetly forth
The freckled cowslip, burnet, and green clover,
Wanting the scythe, all uncorrected, rank,
Conceives by idleness, and nothing teems
But hateful docks, rough thistles, kecksies, burs,
Losing both beauty and utility.
And as our vineyards, fallows, meads, and hedges,
Defective in their natures, grow to wildness,
Even so our houses, and ourselves and children,
Have lost, or do not learn for want of time,
The sciences that should become our country;
But grow, like savages, — as soldiers will,
That nothing do but meditate on blood, —
To swearing, and stern looks, diffus'd attire,
And every thing that seems unnatural.
Which to reduce into our former favour,
You are assembled: and my speech entreats
That I may know the let, why gentle Peace
Should not expel these inconveniences,
And bless us with her former qualities.

KING HENRY

If, Duke of Burgundy, you would the peace,
Whose want gives growth to th'imperfections
Which you have cited, you must buy that peace
With full accord to all our just demands;
Whose tenours and particular effects
You have, enschedul'd briefly, in your hands.

BURGUNDY

The king hath heard them; to the which as yet
There is no answer made.

KING HENRY

              Well, then, the peace,
Which you before so urg'd, lies in his answer.

FRENCH KING

I have but with a cursorary eye
O'erglanc'd the articles: pleaseth your Grace
To appoint some of your council presently
To sit with us once more, with better heed
To re-survey them, we will suddenly
Pass our accept and peremptory answer.

KING HENRY

Brother, we shall. — Go, uncle Exeter, —
And brother Clarence, — and you, brother Gloster, —
Warwick, — and Huntingdon, — go with the king;
And take with you free power to ratify,
Augment, or alter, as your wisdoms best
Shall see advantageable for our dignity,
Any thing in or out of our demands;
And we'll consign thereto. — Will you, fair sister,
Go with the princes, or stay here with us?

QUEEN ISABEL

Our gracious brother, I will go with them:
Haply a woman's voice may do some good,
When articles too nicely urg'd be stood on.

KING HENRY

Yet leave our cousin Katharine here with us:
She is our capital demand, comprised
Within the fore-rank of our articles.

QUEEN ISABEL

She hath good leave.

[*Exeunt all except* KING HENRY,
KATHARINE, *and* ALICE.

KING HENRY

                    Fair Katharine, and most fair!
Will you vouchsafe to teach a soldier terms
Such as will enter at a lady's ear,
And plead his love-suit to her gentle heart?

KATHARINE

Your majesty shall mock at me; I cannot speak your
England.

KING HENRY

O fair Katharine, if you will love me soundly with your
French heart, I will be glad to hear you confess it
brokenly with your English tongue. Do you like me,
Kate?

KATHARINE

Pardonnez-moi, I cannot tell vat is 'like me'.

KING HENRY

An angel is like you, Kate, and you are like an angel.

KATHARINE

Que dit-il? que je suis semblable à les anges?

ALICE

Oui, vraiment, sauf votre grace, ainsi dit-il.

KING HENRY

I said so, dear Katharine; and I must not blush to affirm it.

KATHARINE

*O bon Dieu! les langues des hommes sont pleines de
tromperies.*

KING HENRY

What says she, fair one? that the tongues of men are full
of deceits?

ALICE

Oui, dat de tongues of de mans is be full of deceits —
dat is de princess.

KING HENRY

The princess is the better Englishwoman. I'faith, Kate,
my wooing is fit for thy understanding: I am glad thou
canst speak no better English; for, if thou couldst, thou
wouldst find me such a plain king, that thou wouldst
think I had sold my farm to buy my crown. I know no
ways to mince it in love, but directly to say 'I love you':
then, if you urge me farther than to say, 'Do you in
faith?' I wear out my suit. Give me your answer; i'faith,
do; and so clap hands and a bargain: how say you, lady?

KATHARINE

Sauf votre honneur, me understand vell.

KING HENRY

Marry, if you would put me to verses or to dance for
your sake, Kate, why, you undid me: for the one, I
have neither words nor measure; and for the other, I
have no strength in measure, yet a reasonable measure
in strength. If I could win a lady at leap-frog, or by
vaulting into my saddle with my armour on my back,
under the correction of bragging be it spoken, I should
quickly leap into a wife. Or if I might buffet for my
love, or bound my horse for her favours, I could lay on
like a butcher, and sit like a jack-an-apes, never off.
But, before God, Kate, I cannot look greenly, nor gasp
out my eloquence, nor I have no cunning in
protestation; only downright oaths, which I never use
till urged, nor never break for urging. If thou canst love
a fellow of this temper, Kate, whose face is not worth
sun-burning, that never looks in his glass for love of
any thing he sees there, — let thine eye be thy cook. I
speak to thee plain soldier: if thou canst love me for
this, take me; if not, to say to thee that I shall die, is
true, — but for thy love, by the Lord, no; yet I love
thee too. And while thou livest, dear Kate, take a
fellow of plain and uncoin'd constancy; for he perforce
must do thee right, because he hath not the gift to woo
in other places: for these fellows of infinite tongue, that
can rime themselves into ladies' favours, they do
always reason themselves out again. What! a speaker is
but a prater; a rime is but a ballad. A good leg will fall;
a straight back will stoop; a black beard will turn white;
a curl'd pate will grow bald; a fair face will wither; a
full eye will wax hollow: but a good heart, Kate, is the
sun and the moon; or, rather, the sun, and not the
moon, — for it shines bright, and never changes, but
keeps his course truly. If thou would have such a one,
take me: and take me, take a soldier; take a soldier,
take a king: and what say'st thou, then, to my love?
speak, my fair, and fairly, I pray thee.

KATHARINE

Is it possible dat I sould love de enemy of France?

KING HENRY

No; it is not possible you should love the enemy of
France, Kate: but, in loving me, you should love the
friend of France; for I love France so well, that I will not
part with a village of it; I will have it all mine: and, Kate,
when France is mine and I am yours, then yours is
France and you are mine.

KATHARINE

I cannot tell vat is dat.

KING HENRY

No, Kate? I will tell thee in French; which I am sure will
hang upon my tongue like a new-married wife about her
husband's neck, hardly to be shook off. *Je quand sur le
possession de France, et quand vous avez le possession de
moi,* — let me see, what then? Saint Denis be my speed!
— *donc votre est France et vous êtes mienne.* It is as easy
for me, Kate, to conquer the kingdom, as to speak so
much more French: I shall never move thee in French,
unless it be to laugh at me.

KATHARINE

*Sauf votre honneur, le Français que vous parlez, il est
meilleur que l'Anglais lequel je parle.*

KING HENRY

No, faith, is't not, Kate: but thy speaking of my tongue,
and I thine, most truly-falsely, must needs be granted to
be much at one. But, Kate, dost thou understand thus
much English, — Canst thou love me?

KATHARINE

I cannot tell.

KING HENRY

Can any of your neighbours tell, Kate? I'll ask them.
Come, I know thou lovest me: and at night, when you
come into your closet, you'll question this gentlewoman
about me; and I know, Kate, you will to her dispraise
those parts in me that you love with your heart: but,

good Kate, mock me mercifully; the rather, gentle
princess, because I love thee cruelly. If ever thou beest
mine, Kate, — as I have a saving faith within me tells
me thou shalt, — I get thee with scambling, and thou
must therefore needs prove a good soldier-breeder: shall
not thou and I, between Saint Denis and Saint George,
compound a boy, half French, half English, that shall go
to Constantinople and take the Turk by the beard? shall
we not? what say'st thou, my fair flower-de-luce?

KATHARINE

I do not know dat.

KING HENRY

No; 'tis hereafter to know, but now to promise: do but
now promise, Kate, you will endeavour for your French
part of such a boy; and for my English moiety take the
word of a king and a bachelor. How answer you, *la plus
belle Katharine du monde, mon très-chère et devin déesse?*

KATHARINE

Your majestee ave *fausse* French enough to deceive de
most *sage demoiselle* dat is *en France.*

KING HENRY

Now, fie upon my false French! By mine honour, in true
English, I love thee, Kate: by which honour I dare not
swear thou lovest me; yet my blood begins to flatter me
that thou dost, notwithstanding the poor and
untempering effect of my visage. Now, beshrew my
father's ambition! he was thinking of civil wars when he
got me: therefore was I created with a stubborn outside,
with an aspect of iron, that, when I come to woo ladies,
I fright them. But, in faith, Kate, the elder I wax, the
better I shall appear: my comfort is, that old age, that ill
layer-up of beauty, can do no more spoil upon my face:
thou hast me, if thou hast me, at the worst; and thou
shalt wear me, if thou wear me, better and better: — and
therefore tell me, most fair Katharine, will you have me?
Put off your maiden blushes; avouch the thoughts of
your heart with the looks of an empress; take me by the

hand, and say, 'Henry of England, I am thine': which word thou shalt no sooner bless mine ear withal, but I will tell thee aloud, 'England is thine, Ireland is thine, France is thine, and Henry Plantagenet is thine'; who, though I speak it before his face, if he be not fellow with the best king, thou shalt find the best king of good fellows. Come, your answer in broken music, — for thy voice is music and thy English broken; therefore, queen of all Katharines, break thy mind to me in broken English, — wilt thou have me?

KATHARINE

Dat is as it sall please de *roi mon père*.

KING HENRY

Nay, it will please him well, Kate, — it shall please him, Kate.

KATHARINE

Den it sall also content me.

KING HENRY

Upon that I kiss your hand, and I call you my queen.

KATHARINE

Laissez, mon seigneur, laissez, laissez: ma foi, je ne veux point que vous abaissiez votre grandeur en baisant la main d'une de votre indigne serviteur; excusez-moi, je vous supplie, mon très-puissant seigneur.

KING HENRY

Then I will kiss your lips, Kate.

KATHARINE

Les dames et demoiselles pour être baisées devant leur noces, il n'est pas la coutume de France.

KING HENRY

Madam my interpreter, what says she?

ALICE

Dat it is not be de fashion *pour les* ladies of France, — I cannot tell vat is *baiser en* Anglish.

KING HENRY

To kiss.

ALICE

Your majestee *entendre* bettre *que moi.*

KING HENRY

It is not a fashion for the maids in France to kiss before
they are married, would she say?

ALICE

Oui, vraiment.

KING HENRY

O Kate, nice customs court'sy to great kings. Dear Kate,
you and I cannot be confined within the weak list of a
country's fashion: we are the makers of manners, Kate;
and the liberty that follows our places stops the mouth
of all find-faults, — as I will do yours for upholding the
nice fashion of your country in denying me a kiss:
therefore, patiently and yielding. [*Kissing her.*] You have
witchcraft in your lips, Kate: there is more eloquence in
a sugar touch of them than in the tongues of the French
council; and they should sooner persuade Harry of
England than a general petition of monarchs. — Here
comes your father.

    Enter the French KING *and* QUEEN, BURGUNDY,
        BEDFORD, GLOSTER, EXETER,
     WESTMORELAND, WARWICK, *etc.*

BURGUNDY

God save your majesty! my royal cousin,
Teach you our princess English?

KING HENRY

I would have her learn, my fair cousin, how perfectly I
love her; and that is good English.

BURGUNDY

Is she not apt?

KING HENRY

Our tongue is rough, coz, and my condition is not
smooth; so that, having neither the voice nor the heart
of flattery about me, I cannot so conjure up the spirit of
love in her, that he will appear in his true likeness.

BURGUNDY

Pardon the frankness of my mirth, if I answer you for
that. If you would conjure in her, you must make a
circle; if conjure up love in her in his true likeness, he
must appear naked and blind. Can you blame her, then,
being a maid yet rosed-over with the virgin crimson of
modesty, if she deny the appearance of a naked blind
boy in her naked seeing self? It were, my lord, a hard
condition for a maid to consign to.

KING HENRY

Yet they do wink and yield, — as love is blind and enforces.

BURGUNDY

They are then excused, my lord, when they see not what
they do.

KING HENRY

Then, good my lord, teach your cousin to consent
winking.

BURGUNDY

I will wink on her to consent, my lord, if you will teach
her to know my meaning: for maids, well summer'd and
warm kept, are like flies at Bartholomew-tide, blind,
though they have their eyes; and then they will endure
handling, which before would not abide looking on.

KING HENRY

This moral ties me over to time and a hot summer; and
so I shall catch the fly, your cousin, in the latter end,
and she must be blind too.

BURGUNDY

As love is, my lord, before it loves.

KING HENRY

It is so: and you may, some of you, thank love for my
blindness, who cannot see many a fair French city for
one fair French maid that stands in my way.

FRENCH KING

Yes, my lord, you see them perspectively, the cities
turn'd into a maid; for they are all girdled with maiden
walls that war hath never enter'd.

KING HENRY
Shall Kate be my wife?

FRENCH KING
So please you.

KING HENRY
I am content; so the maiden cities you talk of may wait
on her: so the maid that stood in the way for my wish
shall show me the way to my will.

FRENCH KING
We have consented to all terms of reason.

KING HENRY
Is't so, my lords of England?

WESTMORELAND
The king hath granted every article: —
His daughter first; and then, in sequel, all,
According to their firm proposed natures.

EXETER
Only, he hath not yet subscribed this:
Where your majesty demands, that the King of France,
having any occasion to write for matter of grant, shall
name your highness in this form and with this addition,
in French, *Notre très-cher fils Henri, roi d'Angleterre,
héritier de France*; and thus in Latin, *Præclarissimus filius
noster Henricus, rex Angliæ, et hæres Franciæ.*

FRENCH KING
Nor this I have not, brother, so denied,
But your request shall make me let it pass.

KING HENRY
I pray you, then, in love and dear alliance,
Let that one article rank with the rest;
And thereupon give me your daughter.

FRENCH KING
Take her, fair son; and from her blood raise up
Issue to me; that the contending kingdoms
Of France and England, whose very shores look pale
With envy of each other's happiness,

May cease their hatred; and this dear conjunction
Plant neighbourhood and Christian-like accord
In their sweet bosoms, that never war advance
His bleeding sword 'twixt England and fair France.

ALL

Amen!

KING HENRY

Now, welcome, Kate; — and bear me witness all,
That here I kiss her as my sovereign queen.   [*Flourish.*

QUEEN ISABEL

God, the best maker of all marriages,
Combine your hearts in one, your realms in one!
As man and wife, being two, are one in love,
So be there 'twixt your kingdoms such a spousal,
That never may ill office, or fell jealousy,
Which troubles oft the bed of blessed marriage,
Thrust in between the paction of these kingdoms,
To make divorce of their incorporate league;
That English may as French, French Englishmen,
Receive each other! — God speak this Amen!

ALL

Amen!

KING HENRY

Prepare we for our marriage: — on which day,
My Lord of Burgundy, we'll take your oath,
And all the peers', for surety of our leagues.
Then shall I swear to Kate, and you to me;
And may our oaths well kept and prosperous be!

[*Sennet. Exeunt.*

EPILOGUE

Enter CHORUS.

CHORUS

Thus far, with rough and all unable pen,
  Our bending author hath pursued the story;

In little room confining mighty men,
    Mangling by starts the full course of their glory.
Small time, but in that small, most greatly liv'd
    This star of England: fortune made his sword;
By which the world's best garden be achiev'd,
    And of it left his son imperial lord.
Henry the Sixth, in infant bands crown'd king
    Of France and England, did this king succeed;
Whose state so many had the managing,
    That they lost France, and made his England bleed:
Which oft our stage hath shown; and for their sake,
In your fair minds let this acceptance take.   [*Exit.*

GLOSSARY

References are given only for words having more than one meaning, the first use of each sense being then noted.

Abate, *v.t.* to diminish. M.N.D. III. 2. 432. Deduct, except. L.L.L. V. 2. 539. Cast down. Cor. III. 3. 134. Blunt. R III. V. 5. 35. Deprive. Lear, II. 4. 159.

Abatement, *sb.* diminution Lear, I. 4. 59. Depreciation. Tw.N. I. 1. 13.

Abjects, *sb.* outcasts, servile persons.

Able, *v.t.* to warrant.

Abode, *v.t.* to forebode. 3 H VI. V. 6. 45.

Abode, *sb.* stay, delay. M. of V. II. 6. 77.

Abodements, *sb.* forebodings.

Abram, *adj.* auburn.

Abridgement, *sb.* short entertainment, for pastime.

Abrook, *v.t.* to brook, endure.

Absey book, *sb.* ABC book, or primer.

Absolute, *adj.* resolved. M. for M. III. 1. 5. Positive. Cor. III. 2. 39. Perfect. H V. III. 7. 26. Complete. Tp. I. 2. 109; Lucr. 853.

Aby, *v.t.* to atone for, expiate.

Accite, *v.t.* to cite, summon.

Acknown, *adj.* cognisant.

Acture, *sb.* performance.

Addition, *sb.* title, attribute.

Adoptious, *adj.* given by adoption.

Advice, *sb.* consideration.

Aery, *sb.* eagle's nest or brood. R III. I. 3. 265, 271. Hence generally any brood. Ham. II. 2. 344.

Affectioned, *p.p.* affected.

Affeered, *p.p.* sanctioned, confirmed.

Affiance, *sb.* confidence, trust.

Affined, *p.p.* related. T. & C. I. 3. 25. Bound. Oth. I. 1. 39.

Affront, *v.t.* to confront, meet.

Affy, *v.t.* to betroth. 2 H VI. IV . I. 80. *v.t.* to trust. T.A. I. I. 47.

Aglet-baby, *sb.* small figure cut on the tag of a lace (Fr. *aiguillette*). T. of S. I. 2. 78.

Agnize, *v.t.* to acknowledge, confess.

Agood, *adv.* much.

Aim, *sb.* a guess.

Aim, to cry aim, to encourage, an archery term.

Alderliefest, *adj.* most loved of all.

Ale, *sb.* alehouse.

All amort, completely dejected (Fr. *a la mort*).

Allicholy, *sb.* melancholy.

Allow, *v.t.* to approve.

Allowance, *sb.* acknowledgement, approval.

Ames-ace, *sb.* the lowest throw of the dice.

Anchor, *sb.* anchorite, hermit.

Ancient, *sb.* ensign, standard. I H IV. IV. 2. 32. Ensign, ensign-bearer. I H IV. IV. 2. 24.

Ancientry, *sb.* antiquity, used of old people, W.T. III. 3. 62. Of the gravity which belongs to antiquity, M.A. II. 1. 75.

Angel, *sb.* gold coin, worth about Ios.

Antic, *adj.* fantastic. Ham. I. 5. 172.

Antick, *v.t.* to make a buffoon of. A. & C. II. 7. 126.

Antick, *sb.* buffoon of the old plays.

Appeal, *sb.* impeachment.

Appeal, *v.t.* to impeach.

Apperil, *sb.* peril.

Apple-john, *sb.* a shrivelled winter apple.

Argal, corruption of the Latin *ergo*, therefore.

Argo, corruption of *ergo*, therefore.

Aroint thee, begone, get thee gone.

Articulate, *v.i.* to make articles of peace. Cor. I. 9. 75. *v.t.* to set forth in detail. I H IV. V. I. 72.

Artificial, *adj.* working by art.

Askance, *v.t.* to make look askance or sideways, make to avert.

Aspic, *sb.* asp.

Assured, *p.p.* betrothed.

Atone, *v.t.* to reconcile. R II. I. I. 202. Agree. As V. 4. 112.

Attorney, *sb.* proxy, agent.

Attorneyed, *p.p.* done by proxy. W T. I. 1. 28. Engaged as an attorney, M. for M. V. 1. 383.

Attribute, *sb.* reputation.

Avail, *sb.* profit.

Avise, *v.t.* to inform. Are you avised? = Do you know?

Awful, *adj.* filled with regard for authority.

Awkward, *adj.* contrary.

Baby, *sb.* a doll.

Baccare, go back, a spurious Latin word.

Back-trick, a caper backwards in dancing.

Baffle, *v.t.* to disgrace (a recreant knight).

Bale, *sb.* evil, mischief.

Ballow, *sb.* cudgel.

Ban, *v.t.* curse. 2 H VI. II. 4. 25. *sb.* a curse. Ham. III. 2. 269.

Band, *sb.* bond.

Bank, *v.t.* sail along the banks of.

Bare, *v.t.* to shave.

Barn, *v.t.* to put in a barn.

Barn, or Barne, *sb.* bairn, child.

Base, *sb.* a rustic game. Bid the base = Challenge to a race. Two G. I. 2. 97.

Bases, *sb.* knee-length skirts worn by mounted knights.

Basilisco-like, Basilisco, a character in the play of *Soliman and Perseda*.

Basilisk, *sb.* a fabulous serpent. H V. V. 2. 17. A large cannon. 1 H IV. II. 3. 57.

Bate, *sb.* strife.

Bate, *v.i.* flutter as a hawk. 1 H IV. IV. 1. 99. Diminish. 1 H IV. III. 3. 2.

Bate, *v.t.* abate. Tp. I. 2. 250. Beat down, weaken. M. of V. III. 3. 32.

Bavin, *adj.* made of bavin or brushwood. 1 H IV. III. 2. 61.

Bawbling, *adj.* trifling, insignificant.

Baw-cock, *sb.* fine fellow (Fr. *beau coq*.) H V. III. 2. 25.

Bay, *sb.* space between the main timbers in a roof.

Beadsman, *sb.* one who is hired to offer prayers for another.

Bearing-cloth, *sb.* the cloth in which a child was carried to be christened.

Bear in hand, to deceive with false hopes.

Beat, *v.i.* to meditate. 2 H IV. II. 1. 20. Throb. Lear, III. 4. 14.

Becoming, *sb.* grace.

Beetle, *sb.* a heavy mallet, 2 H IV. I. 2. 235. Beetle-headed = heavy, stupid. T. of S. IV. 1. 150.

Behave, *v.t.* to control.

Behest, *sb.* command.

Behove, *sb.* behoof.

Be-lee'd, *p.p.* forced to lee of the wind.

Bench, *v.i.* to seat on the bench of justice. Lear, III. 6. 38. *v.t.* to elevate to the bench. W.T. I .2. 313.

Bench-hole, the hole of a privy.

Bergomask, a rustic dance, named from Bergamo in Italy.

Beshrew, *v.t.* to curse; but not used seriously.

Besort, *v.t.* to fit, suit.

Bestraught, *adj.* distraught.

Beteem, *v.t.* to permit, grant.

Bezonian, *sb.* a base and needy fellow.

Bias, *adj.* curving like the bias side of a bowling bowl.

Biggen, *sb.* a nightcap.

Bilbo, *sb.* a Spanish rapier, named from Bilbao or Bilboa.

Bilboes, *sb.* stocks used for punishment on shipboard.

Birdbolt, *sb.* a blunt-headed arrow used for birds.

Bisson, *adj.* dim-sighted. Cor. II. 1. 65. Bisson rheum = blinding tears. Ham. II. 2. 514.

Blacks, *sb.* black mourning clothes.

Blank, *sb.* the white mark in the centre of a target.

Blank, *v.t.* to blanch, make pale.

Blanks, *sb.* royal charters left blank to be filled in as occasion dictated.

Blench, *sb.* a swerve, inconsistency.

Blistered, *adj.* padded out, puffed.

Block, *sb.* the wood on which hats are made. M.A. I. 1. 71. Hence, the style of hat. Lear, IV. 6. 185.

Blood-boltered, *adj.* clotted with blood.

Blowse, *sb.* a coarse beauty.

Bob, *sb.* smart rap, jest.

Bob, *v.t.* to beat hard, thwack. R III. V. 3. 335. To obtain by fraud, cheat. T. & C. III. 1. 69.

Bodge, *v.i.* to budge.

Bodkin, *sb.* small dagger, stiletto.

Boggle, *v.i.* to swerve, shy, hesitate.

Boggler, *sb.* swerver.

Boln, *adj.* swollen.

Bolt, *v.t.* to sift, refine.

Bolter, *sb.* a sieve.

Bombard, *sb.* a leathern vessel for liquor.

Bona-robas, *sb.* flashily dressed women of easy virtue.

Bonnet, *v.i.* to doff the hat, be courteous.

Boot, *sb.* profit. 1 H VI. IV. 6. 52. That which is given over and above. R III. IV. 4. 65. Booty. 3 H VI. IV. 1. 13.

Boots, *sb.* Give me not the boots = do not inflict on me the torture of the boots, which were employed to wring confessions.

Bosky, *adj.* woody.

Botcher, *sb.* patcher of old clothes.

Bots, *sb.* small worms in horses.

Bottled, *adj.* big-bellied.

Brabble, *sb.* quarrel, brawl.

Brabbler, *sb.* a brawler.

Brach, *sb.* a hound-bitch.

Braid, *adj.* deceitful.

Braid, *v.t.* to upbraid, reproach.

Brain, *v.t.* to conceive in the brain.

Brazed, *p.p.* made like brass, perhaps hardened in the fire.

Breeched, *p.p.* as though wearing breeches. Mac. II. 3. 120.

Breeching, *adj.* liable to be breeched for a flogging.

Breese, *sb.* a gadfly.

Brib'd-buck, *sb.* perhaps a buck distributed in presents.

Brock, *sb.* badger.

Broken, *adj.* of a mouth with some teeth missing.

Broker, *sb.* agent, go-between.

Brownist, a follower of Robert Brown, the founder of the sect of Independents.

Buck, *v.t.* to wash and beat linen.

Buck-basket, *sb.* a basket to take linen to be bucked.

Bucking, *sb.* washing.

Buckle, *v.i.* to encounter hand to hand, cope. 1. H VI. I. 2. 95. To bow. 2 H VI. I. I. 141.

Budget, *sb.* a leather scrip or bag.

Bug, *sb.* bugbear, a thing causing terror.

Bugle, *sb.* a black bead.

Bully, *sb.* a fine fellow.

Bully-rook, *sb.* a swaggering cheater.

Bung, *sb.* pickpocket.

Burgonet, *sb.* close-fitting Burgundian helmet.

Busky, *adj.* woody.

By-drinkings, *sb.* drinks taken between meals.

Caddis, *sb.* worsted trimming, galloon.

Cade, *sb.* cask, barrel.

Caitiff, *sb.* captive, slave, a wretch. *adj.* R II. I. 2. 53.

Caliver, *sb.* musket.

Callet, *sb.* trull, drab.

Calling, *sb.* appellation.

Calm, *sb.* qualm.

Canaries = quandary.

Canary, *sb.* a lively Spanish dance. *v.i.* to dance canary.

Canker, *sb.* the dog-rose or wild-rose. 1 H IV. I. 3. 176. A worm that destroys blossoms. M.N.D. II. 2.3.

Canstick, *sb.* candlestick.

Cantle, *sb.* piece, slice.

Canton, *sb.* canto.

Canvass, *v.t.* shake as in a sieve, take to task.

Capable, *adj.* sensible. As III. 5. 23. Sensitive, susceptible. Ham. III. 4. 128. Comprehensive. Oth. III. 3. 459. Able to possess. Lear, II. 1. 85.

Capocchia, *sb.* the feminine of capocchio (Ital.), simpleton.

Capriccio, *sb.* caprice, fancy.

Captious, *adj.* either a contraction of capacious or a coined
word meaning capable of receiving.

Carack, *sb.* a large merchant ship.

Carbonado, *sb.* meat scotched for boiling. *v.t.* to hack like a
carbonado.

Card, *sb.* a cooling card = a sudden and decisive stroke.

Card, *v.t.* to mix (liquids).

Cardecu, *sb.* quarter of a French crown (*quart d'écu*).

Care, *v.i.* to take care.

Careire, career, *sb.* a short gallop at full speed.

Carlot, *sb.* peasant.

Carpet consideration, On, used of those made knights for
court services, not for valour in the field.

Carpet-mongers, *sb.* carpet-knights.

Carpets, *sb.* tablecloths.

Case, *v.t.* to strip off the case or skin of an animal. A.W. III.
6. 103. Put on a mask. 1 H IV. II. 2. 55.

Case, *sb.* skin of an animal. Tw.N. V. 1.163. A set, as of
musical instruments, which were in fours. H V. III. 2. 4.

Cashiered, *p.p.* discarded; in M.W.W. I. 1. 168 it probably
means relieved of his cash.

Cataian, *sb.* a native of Cathay, a Chinaman; a cant word.

Cater-cousins, good friends.

Catlings, *sb.* catgut strings for musical instruments.

Cautel, *sb.* craft, deceit, stratagem.

Cautelous, *adj.* crafty, deceitful.

Ceased, *p.p.* put off.

Censure, *sb.* opinion, judgement.

Certify, *v.t.* to inform, make certain.

Cess, *sb.* reckoning; out of all cess = immoderately.

Cesse = cease.

Champain, *sb.* open country.

Channel, *sb.* gutter.

Chape, *sb.* metal end of a scabbard.

Chapless, *adj.* without jaws.

Charact, *sb.* a special mark or sign of office.

Chare, *sb.* a turn of work.

Charge, *sb.* weight, importance. W.T. IV. 3. 258. Cost, expense. John I. 1. 49.

Chaudron, *sb.* entrails.

Check, *sb.* rebuke, reproof.

Check, *v.t.* to rebuke, chide.

Check, *v.i.* to start on sighting game.

Cherry-pit, *sb.* a childish game consisting of pitching cherry-stones into a small hole.

Cheveril, *sb.* leather of kid skin. R. & J. II. 3. 85. *adj.* Tw.N. III. 1. 12.

Che vor ye = I warn you.

Chewet, *sb.* chough. 1 H IV. V. 1. 29. (Fr. *chouette* or *chutte*). Perhaps with play on other meaning of chewet, *i.e.*, a kind of meat pie.

Childing, *adj.* fruitful.

Chop, *v.t.* to clop, pop.

Chopine, *sb.* shoe with a high sole.

Choppy, *adj.* chapped.

Christendom, *sb.* Christian name.

Chuck, *sb.* chick, term of endearment.

Chuff, *sb.* churl, boor.

Cinque pace, *sb.* a slow stately dance. M.A. II. 1. 72. Compare sink-a-pace in Tw.N. I. 3. 126.

Cipher, *v.t.* to decipher.

Circumstance, *sb.* particulars, details. Two G. I. 1. 36. Ceremonious phrases. M. of V. I. 1. 154.

Circumstanced, *p.p.* swayed by circumstance.

Citizen, *adj.* town-bred, effeminate.

Cittern, *sb.* guitar.

Clack-dish, *sb.* wooden dish carried by beggars.

Clamour, *v.t.* to silence.

Clapper-claw, *v.t.* to thrash, drub.

Claw, *v.t.* to scratch, flatter.

Clepe, *v.t.* to call.

Cliff, *sb.* clef, the key in music.

Cling, *v.t.* to make shrivel up.

Clinquant, *adj.* glittering with gold or silver lace or decorations.

Close, *sb.* cadence in music. R II. II. 1. 12. *adj.* secret. T. of S. Ind. I. 127. *v.i.* to come to an agreement, make terms. Two G. II. 5. 12.

Closely, *adv.* secretly.

Clout, *sb.* bull's-eye of a target.

Clouted, *adj.* hobnailed (others explain as patched).

Cobloaf, *sb.* a crusty, ill-shapen loaf.

Cockered, *p.p.* pampered.

Cockle, *sb.* the corncockle weed.

Cockney, *sb.* a city-bred person, a foolish wanton.

Cock-shut time, *sb.* twilight.

Codding, *adj.* lascivious.

Codling, *sb.* an unripe apple.

Cog, *v.i.* to cheat. R III I. 3. 48. *v.t.* to get by cheating, filch. Cor. III. 2. 133.

Coistrel, *sb.* groom.

Collection, *sb.* inference.

Collied, *p.p.* blackened, darkened.

Colour, *sb.* pretext. Show no colour, or bear no colour = allow of no excuse.

Colours, fear no colours = fear no enemy, be afraid of nothing.

Colt, *v.t.* to make a fool of, gull.

Combinate, *adj.* betrothed.

Combine, *v.t.* to bind.

Comfect, *sb.* comfit.

Commodity, *sb.* interest, advantage. John, II. 1. 573. Cargo of merchandise. Tw.N. III. 1. 46.

Comparative, *adj.* fertile in comparisons. 1 H IV. I. 2. 83.

Comparative, *sb.* a rival in wit. 1 H IV. III. 2. 67.

Compassed, *adj.* arched, round.

Complexion, *sb.* temperament.

Comply, *v.i.* to be ceremonious.

Composition, *sb.* agreement, consistency.

Composture, *sb.* compost.

Composure, *sb.* composition. T. & C. II. 3. 238; A. & C. I. 4. 22. Compact. T. & C. II. 3. 100.

Compt. *sb.* account, reckoning.

Comptible, *adj.* susceptible, sensitive.

Con, *v.t.* to study, learn; con thanks = give thanks.

Conceptious, *adj.* apt at conceiving.

Conclusion, *sb.* experiment.

Condolement, *sb.* lamentation. Ham. I. 2. 93. Consolation, Per. II. 1. 150.

Conduce, *v.i.* perhaps to tend to happen.

Conduct, *sb.* guide, escort.

Confiners, *sb.* border peoples.

Confound, *v.t.* to waste. 1 H IV. I. 3. 100. Destroy. M. of V. III. 2. 278.

Congied, *p.p.* taken leave (Fr. *congé*).

Consent, *sb.* agreement, plot.

Consist, *v.i.* to insist.

Consort, *sb.* company, fellowship. Two G. III. 2. 84; IV. I. 64. *v.t.* to accompany. C. of E. I. 2. 28.

Conspectuity, *sb.* power of vision.

Constant, *adj.* consistent.

Constantly, *adv.* firmly, surely.

Conster, *v.t.* to construe, interpret.

Constringed, *p.p.* compressed.

Consul, *sb.* senator.

Containing, *sb.* contents.

Contraction, *sb.* the making of the marriage-contract.

Contrive, *v.t.* to wear out, spend. T. of S. I. 2. 273. Conspire. J.C. II. 3. 16.

Control, *v.t.* to check, contradict.

Convent, *v.t.* to summon.

Convert, *v.i.* to change.

Convertite, *sb.* a penitent.

Convince, *v.t.* to overcome. Mac. I. 7. 64. Convict. T. & C. II. 2. 130.

Convive, *v.i.* to banquet together.

Convoy, *sb.* conveyance, escort.

Copatain hat, *sb.* a high-crowned hat.

Cope, *v.t.* to requite. M. of V. IV. I. 412.

Copesmate, *sb.* a companion.

Copped, *adj.* round-topped.

Copulatives, *sb.* persons desiring to be coupled in marriage.

Copy, *sb.* theme, text. C. of E. V. I. 62. Tenure. Mac. III. 2. 37.

Coranto, *sb.* a quick, lively dance.

Corky, *adj.* shrivelled (with age).

Cornet, *sb.* a band of cavalry.

Corollary, *sb.* a supernumerary.

Cosier, *sb.* botcher, cobbler.

Costard, *sb.* an apple, the head (slang).

Cote, *v.t.* to come up with, pass on the way.

Cot-quean, *sb.* a man who busies himself in women's affairs.

Couch, *v.t.* to make to cower.

Counter, *adv.* to run or hunt counter is to trace the scent of the game backwards.

Counter, *sb.* a metal disk used in reckoning.

Counter-caster, *sb.* one who reckons by casting up counters.

Countermand, *v.t.* to prohibit, keep in check. C. of E. IV. 2. 37. Contradict. Lucr. 276.

Countervail, *v.t.* to outweigh.

County, *sb.* count. As II. I. 67.

Couplet, *sb.* a pair.

Courser's hair, a horse's hair laid in water was believed to turn into a serpent.

Court holy-water, *sb.* flattery.

Courtship, *sb.* courtly manners.

Convent, *sb.* a convent.

Cox my passion = God's passion.

Coy, *v.t.* to fondle, caress. M.N.D. IV. I. 2. *v.i.* to disdain. Cor. V. I. 6.

Crack, *v.i.* to boast. *sb.* an urchin.

Crank, *sb.* winding passage. *v.i.* to wind, twist.

Crants, *sb.* garland, chaplet.

Crare, *sb.* a small sailing vessel.

Crisp, *adj.* curled.

Cross, *sb.* a coin (stamped with a cross).

Cross-row, *sb.* alphabet.

Crow-keeper, *sb.* a boy, or scare-crow, to keep crows from corn.

Cullion, *sb.* a base fellow.

Cunning, *sb.* knowledge, skill. *adj.* knowing, skilful, skilfully wrought.

Curb, *v.i.* to bow, cringe obsequiously.

Curdied, *p.p.* congealed.

Curiosity, *sb.* scrupulous nicety.

Curst, *adj.* bad-tempered.

Curtal, *adj.* having a docked tail. *sb.* a dock-tailed horse.

Customer, *sb.* a loose woman.

Cut, *sb.* a bobtailed horse.

Cuttle, *sb.* a bully.

Daff, *v.t.* to doff. Daff aside = thrust aside slightingly.

Darraign, *v.t.* to arrange, order the ranks for battle.

Dash, *sb.* mark of disgrace.

Daubery, *sb.* false pretence, cheat.

Day-woman, *sb.* dairy-woman.

Debosht, *p.p.* debauched.

Deck, *sb.* pack of cards.

Deem, *sb.* doom; opinion.

Defeat, *v.t.* to disguise. Oth. I. 3. 333. Destroy. Oth. IV. 2. 160.

Defeature, *sb.* disfigurement.

Defend, *v.t.* to forbid.

Defuse, *v.t.* to disorder and make unrecognizable.

Defused, *p.p.* disordered, shapeless.

Demerit, *sb.* desert.

Denier, *sb.* a small French coin.

Dern, *adj.* secret, dismal.

Detect, *v.t.* to discover, disclose.

Determinate, *p.p.* determined upon. Tw.N. II. 1. 10. Decided. Oth. IV. 2. 229. Ended. Sonn. LXXXVII. 4. *v.t.* bring to an end. R II. I. 3.

Dich, *v.i.* do to, happen to.

Diet, *v.t.* keep strictly, as if by a prescribed regimen.

Diffidence, *sb.* distrust, suspicion.

Digression, *sb.* transgression.

Diminutives, *sb.* the smallest of coins.

Directitude, *sb.* a blunder for some word unknown. Cor. IV. 5. 205.

Disanimate, *v.t.* to discourage.

Disappointed, *p.p.* unprepared.

Discandy, *v.i.* to thaw, melt.

Discipled, *p.p.* taught.

Disclose, *v.t.* to hatch. *sb.* the breaking of the shell by the chick on hatching.

Disme, *sb.* a tenth.

Distain, *v.t.* to stain, pollute.

Dive-dapper, *sb.* dabchick.

Dividant, *adj.* separate, different.

Dotant, *sb.* dotard.

Doubt, *sb.* fear, apprehension.

Dout, *v.t.* to extinguish.

Dowlas, *sb.* coarse linen.

Dowle, *sb.* down, the soft plumage of a feather.

Down-gyved, *adj.* hanging down about the ankle like gyves.

Dribbling, *adj.* weakly shot.

Drugs, *sb.* drudges.

Drumble, *v.i.* to be sluggish or clumsy.

Dry-beat, *v.t.* to cudgel, thrash.

Dry-foot. To draw dry-foot, track by scent.

Dudgeon, *sb.* the handle of a dagger.

Due, *v.t.* to endue.

Dump, *sb.* a sad strain.

Dup, *v.t.* to open.

Ean, *v.i.* to yean, lamb.

Ear, *v.t.* to plough, till.

Eche, *v.t.* to eke out.

Eftest, *adv.* readiest.

Eftsoons, *adv.* immediately.

Egal, *adj.* equal.

Egally, *adv.* equally.

Eisel, *sb.* vinegar.

Elf, *v.t.* to mat hair in a tangle; believed to be the work of elves.

Emballing, *sb.* investiture with the crown and sceptre.

Embarquement, *sb.* hindrance, restraint.

Ember-eyes, *sb.* vigils of Ember days.

Embowelled, *p.p.* emptied, exhausted.

Emmew, *v.t.* perhaps to mew up.

Empiricutic, *adj.* empirical, quackish.

Emulation, *sb.* jealous rivalry.

Enacture, *sb.* enactment, performance.

Encave, *v.t.* to hide, conceal.

Encumbered, *p.p.* folded.

End, *sb.* still an end = continually.

End, *v.t.* to get in the harvest.

Englut, *v.t.* to swallow.

Enlargement, *sb.* liberty, liberation.

Enormous, *adj.* out of the norm, monstrous.

Enseamed, *p.p.* defiled, filthy.

Ensear, *v.t.* to sear up, make dry.

Enshield, *adj.* enshielded, protected.

Entertain, *v.t.* to take into one's service.

Entertainment, *sb.* service.

Entreat, *v.t.* to treat.

Entreatments, *sb.* invitations.

Ephesian, *sb.* boon companion.

Eryngoes, *sb.* roots of the sea-holly, a supposed aphrodisiac.

Escot, *v.t.* to pay for.

Espial, *sb.* a spy.

Even Christian, *sb.* fellow Christian.

Excrement, *sb.* anything that grows out of the body, as hair, nails, etc. Used of the beard. M. of V. III. 2. 84. Of the hair. C. of E. II. 2. 79. Of the moustache. L.L.L. V. I. 98.

Exhibition, *sb.* allowance, pension.

Exigent, *sb.* end. 1 H VI. II. 5. 9. Exigency, critical need. J. C. V. I. 19.

Exion, *sb.* blunder for action.

Expiate, *v.t* . to terminate. Sonn. XXII. 4.

Expiate, *p.p.* ended. R III. III. 3. 24.

Exsufflicate, *adj.* inflated, both literally and metaphorically.

Extent, *sb.* seizure. As III. 1. 17. Violent attack. Tw.N. IV. 1. 51. Condescension, favour. Ham. II. 2. 377. Display. T. A. IV. 4. 3.

Extraught, *p.p.* extracted.

Extravagancy, *sb.* vagrancy, aimless wandering about.

Eyas, *sb.* a nestling, a young hawk just taken from the nest.

Eyas-musket, *sb.* the young sparrow-hawk.

Eye, *v.i.* to appear, look to the eye.

Facinerious, *adj.* wicked.

Fadge, *v.i.* to succeed, suit.

Fading, *sb.* the burden of a song.

Fair, *v.t.* to make beautiful.

Fairing, *sb.* a gift.

Faitor, *sb.* evil-doer.

Fangled, *adj.* fond of novelties.

Fap, *adj.* drunk.

Farced, *p.p.* stuffed out.

Fardel, *sb.* a burden, bundle.

Fat, *adj.* cloying. *sb.* vat.

Favour, *sb.* outward appearance, aspect. In pl. = features.

Fear, *v.t.* to frighten. 3 H VI. III. 3. 226. Fear for. M. of V. III. 5. 3.

Feat, *adj.* neat, dexterous.

Feat, *v.t.* to fashion, form.

Fee, *sb.* worth, value.

Feeder, *sb.* servant.

Fee-farm, *sb.* a tenure without limit of time.

Fellowly, *adj.* companionable, sympathetic.

Feodary, *sb.* confederate.

Fere, *sb.* spouse, consort.

Ferret, *v.t.* to worry.

Festinate, *adj.* swift, speedy.

Fet, *p.p.* fetched.

Fico, *sb.* a fig (Span.).

File, *sb.* list.

File, *v.t.* to defile. Mac. III. 1. 65. Smooth, polish. L.L.L. V. 1. 11. *v.i.* to walk in file. H VIII. III. 2. 171.

Fill-horse, *sb.* a shaft-horse.

Fills, *sb.* shafts.

Fineless, *adj.* endless, infinite.

Firago, *sb.* virago.

Firk, *v.t.* to beat.

Fitchew, *sb.* pole-cat.

Fitment, *sb.* that which befits.

Flap-dragon, *sb.* snap-dragon, or small burning object, lighted and floated in a glass of liquor, to be swallowed burning. L.L.L. V. 1. 43. 2 H IV. II. 4. 244. *v.t.* to swallow like a flap-dragon. W.T. III. 3.100.

Flaw, *sb.* gust of wind. Ham. V. 1. 223. Small flake of ice. 2 H IV. IV. 4. 35. Passionate outburst. M. for M. II. 3. 11. A crack. Lear, II. 4. 288. *v.t.* make a flaw in, break. H VIII. I. 1. 95; I. 2. 21.

Fleer, *sb.* sneer. Oth. IV. 1. 83. *v.i.* to grin; sneer. L.L.L. V. 2. 109.

Fleshment, *sb.* encouragement given by first success.

Flewed, *p.p.* with large hanging chaps.

Flight, *sb.* a long light arrow.

Flighty, *adj.* swift.

Flirt-gill, *sb.* light wench.

Flote, *sb.* sea.

Flourish, *v.t.* to ornament, gloss over.

Fobbed, *p.p.* cheated, deceived.

Foil, *sb.* defeat. 1 H VI. III. 3. 11. *v.t.* to defeat, mar. Pass. P. 99

Foin, *v.i.* to thrust (in fencing).

Fopped, *p.p.* cheated, fooled.

Forbod, *p.p.* forbidden.

Fordo, *v.t.* to undo, destroy.

Foreign, *adj.* dwelling abroad.

Fork, *sb.* the forked tongue of a snake. M. for M. III. 1. 16. The barbed head of an arrow. Lear, I. 1. 146. The junction of the legs with the trunk. Lear, IV. 6. 120.

Forked, *p.p.* barbed. As II. 1. 24. Horned as a cuckold. T. & C. I. 2. 164.

Forslow, *v.i.* to delay.

Forspeak, *v.t.* to speak against.

Fosset-seller, *sb.* a seller of taps.

Fox, *sb.* broadsword.

Foxship, *sb.* selfish and ungrateful, cunning.

Fracted, *p.p.* broken.

Frampold, *adj.* turbulent, quarrelsome.

Frank, *v.t.* to pen in a frank or sty. R III. 1. 3. 314. *sb.* a sty. 2 H IV. II. 2. 145. *adj.* liberal. Lear, III. 4. 20.

Franklin, *sb.* a yeoman.

Fraught, *sb.* freight, cargo, load. Tw.N. V. 1. 59. *v.t.* to load, burden. Cym. I. 1. 126. *p.p.* laden. M. of V. II. 8. 30. Stored. Two G. III. 2. 70.

Fraughtage, *sb.* cargo. C. of E. IV. 1. 8.

Fraughting, *part. adj.* constituting the cargo.

Frize, *sb.* a kind of coarse woollen cloth with a nap.

Frontier, *sb.* an outwork in fortification. 1 H IV. II. 3. 56. Used figuratively. 1 H IV. I. 3. 19.

Fruitful, *adj.* bountiful, plentiful.

Frush, *v.t.* to bruise, batter.

Frutify, blunder for certify. M. of V II. 2. 132.

Fubbed off, *p.p.* put off with excuses. 2 H IV. II. 1. 34.

Fullams, *sb.* a kind of false dice.

Gad, *sb.* a pointed instrument. T.A. IV. 1. 104. Upon the gad = on the spur of the moment, hastily. Lear, I. 2. 26.

Gage, *v.t.* to pledge.

Gaingiving, *sb.* misgiving.

Galliard, *sb.* a lively dance.

Gallimaufry, *sb.* medley, tumble.

Gallow, *v.t.* to frighten.

Gallowglass, *sb.* heavy- armed Irish foot-soldier.

Gallows, *sb.* a rogue, one fit to be hung.

Gallows-bird, *sb.* one that merits hanging.

Garboil, *sb.* uproar, commotion.

Gaskins, *sb.* loose breeches.

Gastness, *sb.* ghastliness, terror.

Geck, *sb.* dupe.

Generation, *sb.* offspring.

Generous, *adj.* nobly born.

Gennet, *sb.* a Spanish horse.

Gentry, *sb.* rank by birth. M.W. W. II. 1. 51. Courtesy. Ham. II. 2. 22.

German, *sb.* a near kinsman.

Germen, *sb.* germ, seed.

Gest, *sb.* a period of sojourn; originally the halting place in a royal progress.

Gib, *sb.* an old rom-cat.

Gibbet, *v.t.* to hang, as a barrel when it is slung.

Gig, *sb.* top.

Giglot, *adj.* wanton. 1 H VI. IV. 7. 41. *sb.* M. for M. V. 1. 345.

Gillyvors, *sb.* gillyflowers.

Gimmal-bit, *sb.* a double bit, or one made with double rings.

Gimmer, *sb.* contrivance, mechanical device.

Ging, *sb.* gang, pack.

Gird, *sb.* a scoff, jest. 2 H VI. III. 1. 131. *v.t.* to taunt, gibe at. 2 H IV. I. 2. 6.

Gleek, *sb.* scoff. 1 H VI. IV. 2. 12. *v.i.* to scoff. M.N.D. III. 1. 145.

Glib, *v.t.* to geld.

Gloze, *v.i.* to comment. H V. I. 2. 40. T. & C. II. 2. 165. To use flattery. R II. II. 1. 10; T.A. IV. 4. 35.

Gnarling, *pr.p.* snarling.

Godden, *sb.* good den, good even.

God'ild, God yield, God reward.

God-jer = good-year.

Good-year, *sb.* a meaningless interjection. M.A. I. 3. 1. Some malific power. Lear, V. 3. 24.

Goss, *sb.* gorse.

Gossip, *sb.* sponsor. Two G. III. 1. 269. *v.t.* to stand sponsor for. A. W. I. 1. 176.

Gorbellied, *adj.* big-bellied.

Graff, *sb.* graft, scion. *v.t.* to graft.

Grain, *sb.* a fast colour. Hence in grain = ingrained.

Gratillity, *sb.* gratuity.

Gratulate, *adj.* gratifying.

Greek, *sb.* boon companion.

Grise, *sb.* a step.

Guard, *v.t.* to trim, ornament.

Guardant, *sb.* sentinel, guard.

Guidon, *sb.* standard, banner.

Gules, *adj.* red, in heraldry.

Gust, *sb.* taste. *v.t.* to taste.

Hackney, *sb.* loose woman.

Haggard, *sb.* untrained hawk.

Haggled, *p.p.* hacked, mangled.

Hair, *sb.* texture, nature. 1 H IV. IV. 1. 61. Against the hair = against the grain. R. & J. II. 3. 97.

Handfast, *sb.* betrothal, contract. Cym. I. 5. 78. Custody. W.T. IV. 3. 778.

Handsaw, *sb.* corruption of heronshaw, a heron.

Hardiment, *sb.* daring deed.

Harlot, *adj.* lewd, base.

Hatched, *p.p.* closed with a hatch or half door. Per. IV. 2. 33. Engraved. T. & C. I. 3. 65.

Havoc, to cry havoc = cry no quarter. John, II. 1. 357. *v.t.* cut to pieces, destroy. H V. I. 2. 193.

Hawking, *adj.* hawk-like.

Hay, *sb.* a round dance. L.L.L. V. I. 147. A term in fencing when a hit is made (Ital. *hai*, you have it). R. & J. II. 4. 27.

Hebenon, *sb.* perhaps the yew (Germ. *Eiben*). Ebony and henbane have been suggested.

Hefts, *sb.* heavings.

Helm, *v.t.* to steer.

Helpless, *adj.* not helping, useless. R III. I. 2. 13; Lucr. 1027. Incurable, Lucr. 756.

Hent, *sb.* grasp, hold. Ham. III. 3. 88. *v.t.* to hold, pass. M. for M. IV. 6. 14.

Hermit, *sb.* beadsman, one bound to pray for another.

Hild = held.

Hilding, *sb.* a good-for-nothing.

Hoar, *adj.* mouldy, R. & J. II. 3. 136. *v.i.* to become mouldy. R. & J. II. 3. 142.

Hoar, *v.t.* to make hoary or white, as with leprosy.

Hobby-horse, *sb.* a principal figure in the old morris dance. L.L.L. III. I. 30. A light woman. M.A. III. 2. 68.

Hob-nob, have or not have, hit or miss.

Hold in, *v.i.* to keep counsel.

Holding, *sb.* the burden of a song. A. & C. II. 7. 112. Fitness, sense. A.W. IV. 2. 27.

Holy-ales, *sb.* rural festivals.

Honest, *adj.* chaste.

Honesty, *sb.* chastity. M.W.W. II. 2. 234. Decency. Tw.N. II. 3. 85. Generosity, liberality. Tim. III. 1. 30.

Honey-seed, blunder for homicide, 2 H IV. II. I. 52.

Honey-suckle, blunder for homicidal. 2 H IV. II. I. 50.

Hoodman, *sb.* the person blinded in the game of hoodman-blind.

Hoodman-blind, *sb.* blind-man's buff.

Hot at hand, not to be held in.

Hot-house, *sb.* bagnio, often in fact a brothel as well.

Hox, *v.t.* to hough, hamstring.

Hoy, *sb.* a small coasting vessel.

Hugger-mugger, In, stealthily and secretly.

Hull, *v.i.* to float.

Hulling, *pr. p.* floating at the mercy of the waves.

Ignomy, *sb.* ignominy.

Imbar, *v.t.* to bar in, make secure. H V. I. 2. 94.

Imboss, *v.t.* to hunt to death.

Imbossed, *p.p.* swollen. As II. 7. 67. Foaming at the mouth. T. of S. Ind. I. 16.

Immanity, *sb.* savageness, ferocity.

Immoment, *adj.* insignificant.

Immures, *sb.* surrounding walls.

Imp, *v.t.* to graft new feathers to a falcon's wing.

Impair, *adj.* unsuitable.

Impale, *v.t.* to encircle.

Impart, *v.t.* to afford, grant. Lucr. 1039; Sonn. LXXII. 8. *v.i.* to behave oneself. Ham. I. 2. 112.

Imperceiverant, *adj.* lacking in perception.

Impeticos, *v.t.* to put in the petticoat or pocket.

Importance, *sb.* importunity. John, II. 1. 7. Import. W.T. V. 2. 19. Question at issue, that which is imported. Cym. I. 5. 40.

Imposition, *sb.* command, injunction. M. of V. I. 2. 106. Penalty. M. for M. I. 2. 186.

Imposthume, *sb.* abscess.

Imprese, *sb.* device with a motto.

Include, *v.t.* to conclude, end.

Incontinent, *adj.* immediate.

Incony, *adj.* dainty, delicate.

Indent, *v.i.* to make terms.

Index, *sb.* introduction (in old books the index came first).

Indifferency, *sb.* impartiality.

Indirectly, *adv.* wrongly, unjustly.

Indurance, *sb.* durance, imprisonment.

Infest, *v.t.* to vex, trouble.

Inherit, *v.t.* to possess. Tp. IV. 1. 154. To cause to possess, put in possession. R II. I. 1. 85. *v.i.* to take possession. Tp. II. 2. 182.

Inheritor, *sb.* possessor.

Injury, *sb.* insult.

Inkhorn mate, *sb.* bookworm.

Inkle, *sb.* coarse tape.

Insisture, *sb.* persistence.

Intenible, *adj.* incapable of holding.

Intention, *sb.* aim, direction.

Intermissive, *adj.* intermitted, interrupted.

Intrinse, *adj.* tightly drawn.

Invised, *adj.* unseen, a doubtful word.

Irregulous, *adj.* lawless.

Jack, *sb.* figure that struck the bell in old clocks. R III. IV. 2. 114. A term of contempt. R III. I. 3. 72. The small bowl aimed at in the game of bowls. Cym. II. 1. 2. The key of a virginal. Sonn. CXXVIII. 5. A drinking vessel. T. of S. IV. 1. 48.

Jade, *v.t.* to play the jade with, run away with. Tw.N. II. 5. 164. Drive like a jade. A. & C. III. 1. 34. Treat with contempt. H VIII. III. 2. 280.

Jakes, *sb.* a privy.

Jar, *sb.* a tick of the clock. W.T. I. 2. 43.

Jar, *v.t.* to tick. R II. V. 5. 51. *v.i.* to guard. 1 H VI. III. 1. 70. *sb.* a quarrel. 1 H VI. I. 1. 44.

Jesses, *sb.* straps attaching the legs of a hawk to the fist.

Jet, *v.i.* to strut. Tw.N. II. 4. 32. Advance threateningly. R III. II. 4. 51.

Journal, *adj.* diurnal, daily.

Jowl, *v.t.* to knock, dash.

Kam, *adj.* crooked, away from the point.

Keech, *sb.* a lump of tallow or fat.

Keel, *v.t.* to cool.

Ken, *sb.* perception, sight. *v.t.* to know.

Kern, *sb.* light-armed foot-soldier of Ireland.

Kibe, *sb.* chilblain on the heel.

Kicky-wicky, *sb.* a pet name.

Killen = to kill.

Kiln-hole, *sb.* the fireplace of an oven or kiln.

Kind, *sb.* nature. M. of V. I. 3. 84. *adj.* natural. Lucr. 1423. *adv.* kindly. Tim. I. 2. 224.

Kindle, *v.t.* to bring forth young. As III. 2. 343. Incite. As I. 1. 179.

Knack, *sb.* a pretty trifle.

Knap, *v.t.* to gnaw, nibble. M. of V. III. 1. 9. Rap. Lear, II. 4. 123.

Laboursome, *adj.* elaborate.

Laced mutton, *sb.* slang for courtesan.

Lade, *v.t.* to empty, drain.

Land-damn. Unrecognizably corrupt word in W.T. II. 1. 143.

Lapsed, *p.p.* caught, surprised. Tw.N. III. 3. 36.

Latch, *v.t.* to catch, lay hold of.

Latten, *sb.* a mixture of copper and tin. M.W.W. I. 1. 153.

Laund, *sb.* glade.

Lavolt, *sb.* a dance in which two persons bound high and whirl round.

Lay for, *v.t.* to strive to win.

Leasing, *sb.* lying, falsehood.

Leave, *sb.* liberty, license.

Leer, *sb.* complexion.

Leese, *v.t.* to lose.

Leet, *sb.* a manor court. T. of S. Ind. II. 87. The time when such is held. Oth. III. 3. 140.

Leiger, *sb.* ambassador.

Length, *sb.* delay.

Let, *v.t.* to hinder. Tw.N. V. 1. 246; Ham. I. 4. 85. Detain. W.T. I. 2. 41. Forbear. Lucr. 10. *p.p.* caused. Ham. IV. 6. 11. *sb.* hindrance. H V. V. 2. 65.

Let-alone, *sb.* hindrance, prohibition.

Level, *sb.* aim, line of fire. R. & J. III. 3. 102. *v.i.* to aim. R III. IV. 4. 202. Be on the same level. Oth. I. 3. 239. *adv.* evenly. Tw.N. II. 4. 32.

Lewd, *adj.* base, vile.

Libbard, *sb.* leopard.

Liberal, *adj*. licentious. Liberal conceit = elaborate design. Ham. V. 2. 152. *adv*. freely, openly. Oth. V. 2. 220.

Lieger, *sb*. ambassador.

Lifter, *sb*. thief.

Light, *p.p*. lighted.

Likelihood, *sb*. sign, indication.

Lime, *v.t*. to put lime into liquor. M.W.W. I. 3. 14. Smear with bird-lime. 2 H VI. I. 3. 86. Catch with bird-lime. Tw.N. III. 4. 75. Cement. 3 H VI. V. I. 84.

Limit, *sb*. appointed time. R II. I. 3. 151. *v.t*. to appoint. John. V. 2. 123.

Line, *v.t*. to draw, paint. As III. 2. 93. Strengthen, fortify. 1 H IV. II. 3. 85.

Line-grove, *sb*. a grove of lime trees.

Linsey-woolsey, *sb*. gibberish (literally, mixed stuff).

Lipsbury pinfold. Perhaps = between the teeth.

List, *sb*. desire, inclination. Oth. II. 1. 105. Limit, boundary. 1 H IV. IV. 1. 51. Lists for combat. Mac. III. 1. 70.

Lither, *adj*. flexible, gentle.

Livery, *sb*. delivery of a freehold into the possession of the heir.

Lob, *sb*. lubber, lout.

Lockram, *sb*. coarse linen.

Lodge, *v.t*. to lay flat, beat down.

Loggats, *sb*. a game somewhat resembling bowls.

Loof, *v.t*. to luff, bring close to the wind.

Losel, *sb*. a wasteful, worthless fellow.

Lout, *v.t*. to make a lout or fool of.

Lown, *sb*. base fellow.

Luce, *sb*. pike or jack.

Lurch, *v.t*. to win a love set at a game; bear off the prize easily. Cor. II. 2. 102. *v.i*. to skulk. M. W. W. II. 2. 25.

Lym, *sb*. bloodhound; so called from the leam or leash used to hold him.

Maggot-pie, *sb*. magpie.

Main, *sb*. a call at dice. 1 H IV. IV. 1. 47. Mainland. Lear, III. 1. 6. The chief power. Ham. V. 4. 15.

Main-course, *sb.* mainsail.

Main'd, *p.p.* maimed.

Makeless, *adj.* mateless, widowed.

Malkin, *sb.* slattern.

Mallard, *sb.* a wild drake.

Mallecho, *sb.* mischief (Span. *malhecho*).

Malt-horse, *sb.* brewer's horse.

Mammering, *pr.p.* hesitating.

Mammet, *sb.* a doll.

Mammock, *v.t.* to tear in pieces.

Manakin, *sb.* little man.

Mankind, *adj.* masculine, applied to a woman.

Manner, with the = in the act, red-handed.

Mare, *sb.* nightmare. To ride the wild mare = play at see-saw.

Mark, *sb.* thirteen shillings and fourpence.

Mart, *v.i.* to market, traffic. Cym. I. 6. 150. *v.t.* to vend, traffic with. J. C. IV. 3. 11.

Mastic, *sb.* used to stop decayed teeth.

Match, *sb.* compact, bargain. M. of V. III. 1. 40. Set a match = make an appointment. 1 H IV. 1. 2. 110.

Mate, *v.t.* to confound, make bewildered. C. of E. III. 2. 54. Match, cope with. H VIII. III. 2. 274.

Material, *adj.* full of matter.

Maugre, *prep.* in spite of.

Maund, *sb.* a basket.

Mazard, *sb.* skull.

Meacock, *adj.* spiritless, pusillanimous.

Mealed. *p.p.* mingled, compounded.

Mean, *sb.* the intermediate part between the tenor and treble.

Meiny, *sb.* attendants, retinue.

Mell, *v.i.* to meddle.

Mered, He being the mered question—the question concerning him alone. A. & C. III. 13. 10.

Mess, *sb*, a set of four. L.L.L. IV. 3. 204. Small quantity. 2 H IV. II. 1. 95. Lower messes = inferiors, as messing at the lower end of the table. W.T. I. 2. 226.

Mete, *v. i.* to mete at = aim at.

Metheglin, *sb.* a kind of mead, made of honey and water.

Micher, *sb.* truant.

Miching, *adj.* sneaking, stealthy.

Mineral, *sb.* a mine.

Minikin, *adj.* small, pretty.

Minion, *sb.* darling, favourite. John, II. 1. 392. Used contemptuously. 2 H VI. I. 3. 82. A pert, saucy person. 2 H VI. I. 3. 136.

Mirable, *adj.* admirable.

Mire, *v.i.* to be bemired, sink as into mire.

Misdread, *sb.* fear of evil.

Misprision, *sb.* mistake. M.N.D. III. 2. 90. Contempt. A.W. II. 3. 153.

Misproud, *adj.* viciously proud.

Miss, *sb.* misdoing.

Missingly, *adv.* regretfully.

Missive, *sb.* messenger.

Misthink, *v.t.* to misjudge.

Mobled, *p.p.* having the face or head muffled.

Modern, *adj.* commonplace, trite.

Module, *sb.* mould, form.

Moldwarp, *sb.* mole.

Mome, *sb.* blockhead, dolt.

Momentany, *adj.* momentary, lasting an instant.

Monster, *v.t.* to make monstrous.

Month's mind, *sb.* intense desire or yearning.

Moralize, *v.t.* to interpret, explain.

Mort, *sb.* trumpet notes blown at the death of the deer.

Mortal, *adj.* deadly.

Mortified, *p.p.* deadened, insensible.

Mot, *sb.* motto, device.

Mother, *sb.* the disease *hysterica passio*.

Motion, *v.t.* to propose, counsel. 1 H VI. I. 3. 63. *sb.* a puppet show. W.T. IV. 3. 96. A puppet. Two G. II. 1. 91. Solicitation, proposal, suit. C. of E. I. 1. 60. Emotion, feeling, impulse. Tw.N. II. 4. 18.

Motive, *sb.* a mover, instrument, member.

Mountant, *adj.* lifted up.

Mow, *sb.* a grimace. *v.i.* to grimace.

Moy, *sb.* probably some coin.

Muleter, *sb. muleteer.*

Mulled, *p.p.* flat, insipid.

Mummy, *sb.* a medical or magical preparation originally made from mummies.

Murdering-piece, *sb.* a cannon loaded with chain-shot.

Murrion, *adj.* infected with the murrain.

Muse, *v.i.* to wonder. John, III. 1. 317. *v.t.* to wonder at. Tp. III. 3. 36.

Muset, *sb.* a gap or opening in a hedge.

Muss, *sb.* scramble.

Mutine, *sb.* mutineer.

Mystery, *sb.* profession. M. for M. IV. 2. 28. Professional skill. A.W. III. 6. 65.

Nayword, *sb.* pass-word, M.W.W. II. 2. 126. A by-word. Tw.N. II. 3. 132.

Neat, *adj.* trim, spruce.

Neb, *sb.* bill or beak.

Neeld, *sb.* needle.

Neeze, *v.i.* to sneeze.

Neif, *sb.* fist.

Next, *adj.* nearest.

Nick, *sb.* out of all nick, beyond all reckoning.

Night-rule, *sb.* revelry.

Nill = will not.

Nine-men's-morris, *sb.* a rustic game.

Note, *sb.* list, catalogue. W.T. IV. 2. 47. Note of expectation = list of expected guests. Mac. III. 3. 10. Stigma, mark of reproach. R II. I. 1. 43. Distinction. Cym. II. 3. 12. knowledge, observation. Lear, III. 1. 18.

Nott-pated, *adj.* crop-headed.

Nousle, *v.t.* to nurse, nourish delicately.

Nowl, *sb.* noddle.

Nuthook, *sb.* slang for catchpole.

Oathable, *adj.* capable of taking an oath.

Object, *sb.* anything presented to the sight; everything that comes in the way.

Obsequious, *adj.* regardful of funeral rites. 3 H VI. II. 5. 118. Funereal, having to do with obsequies. T. A. V. 3. 153.

Observance, *sb.* observation. Oth. III. 3. 151. Homage. 2 H IV. IV. 3. 15. Ceremony. M. of V. II. 2. 194.

Obstacle, *sb.* blunder for obstinate.

Occupation, *sb.* trade (in contemptuous sense). Cor. IV. 1. 14. Voice of occupation = vote of working men. Cor. IV. 6. 98.

Odd, *adj.* unnoticed. Tp. I. 2. 223. At odds. T. & C. IV. 5. 265.

Oeillades, *sb.* amorous glances.

O' ergrown, *p.p.* bearded. Cym. IV. 4. 33. Become too old. M. for M. I. 3. 22.

O'erstrawed, *p.p.* overstrewn.

Office, *v.t.* to office all = do all the domestic service. A. W. III. 2. 128. Keep officiously. Cor. V. 2. 61.

Oneyers, *sb.* unexplained word.

Opposition, *sb.* combat, encounter.

Orb, *sb.* orbit. R. & J. II. 1. 151. Circle. M.N.D. II. 1. 9. A heavenly body. M. of V. V. 1. 60. The earth. Tw.N. III. 1. 39.

Ordinant, *adj.* ordaining, controlling.

Ordinary, *sb.* a public dinner at which each man pays for his own share.

Ort, *sb.* remnant, refuse.

Ouphs, *sb.* elves, goblins.

Outrage, *sb.* outburst of rage.

Overscutch'd, *p.p.* over-whipped, over-switched (perhaps in a wanton sense).

Overture, *sb.* disclosure. W.T. II. 1. 172. Declaration. Tw.N. I. 5. 208.

Owe, *v.t.* to own, possess.

Packing, *sb.* plotting, conspiracy.

Paddock, *sb.* toad. Ham. III. 4. 191. A familiar spirit in the form of a toad. Mac. I. 1. 9.

Pajock, *sb.* term of contempt, by some said to mean peacock.

Pale, *sb.* enclosure, confine.

Palliament, *sb.* robe.

Parcel-bawd, *sb.* half-bawd.

Paritor, *sb.* apparitor, an officer of the Bishops' Court.

Part, *sb.* party, side.

Partake, *v.t.* to make to partake, impart. W.T. V. 3. 132. To share. J.C. II. 1. 305.

Parted, *p.p.* endowed.

Partisan, *sb.* a kind of pike.

Pash, *sb.* a grotesque word for the head. W.T. I. 2. 128. *v.t.* to smite, dash. T. & C. II. 3. 202.

Pass, *v.t.* to pass sentence on. M. for M. II. 1. 19. Care for. 2 H VI. IV. 2. 127. Represent. L.L.L. V. 1. 123. Make a thrust in fencing. Tw.N. III. 1. 44.

Passage, *sb.* passing to and fro. C. of E. III. 1. 99. Departure, death. Ham. III. 3. 86. Passing away. 1 H VI. II. 5. 108. Occurrence. A.W. I. 1. 19. Process, course. R. & J. Prol. 9. Thy passages of life = the actions of thy life. 1 H IV. III. 2. 8. Passages of grossness = gross impositions. Tw.N. III. 2. 70. Motion. Cor. V. 6. 76.

Passant. In heraldry, the position of an animal walking.

Passion, *sb.* passionate poem. M.N.D. V. 1. 306; Sonn. XX. 2.

Passionate, *v.t.* to express with emotion. T.A. III. 2. 6. *adj.* displaying emotion. 2 H VI. I. 1. 104. Sorrowful. John, II. 1. 544.

Passy measures, a corruption of the Italian *passamezzo*, denoting a stately and measured step in dancing.

Patch, *sb.* fool.

Patchery, *sb.* knavery, trickery.

Patronage, *v.t.* to patronize, protect.

Pavin, *sb.* a stately dance of Spanish or Italian origin.

Pawn, *sb.* a pledge.

Peach, *v.t.* to impeach, accuse.

Peat, *sb.* pet, darling.

Pedascule, *sb.* vocative, pedant, schoolmaster.

Peevish, *adj.* childish, silly. 1 H VI. V. 3. 186. Fretful, wayward. M. of V. I. 1. 86.

Peise, *v.t.* to poise, balance. John, II. 1. 575. Retard by making heavy. M. of V. III. 2. 22. Weigh down. R III. V. 3. 106.

Pelt, *v.i.* to let fly with words of opprobrium.

Pelting, *adj.* paltry.

Penitent, *adj.* doing penance.

Periapt, *sb.* amulet.

Period, *sb.* end, conclusion. A. & C. IV. 2. 25. *v.t.* to put an end to. Tim. I. 1. 103.

Perked up, *p.p.* dressed up.

Perspective, *sb.* glasses so fashioned as to create an optical illusion.

Pert, *adj.* lively, brisk.

Pertaunt-like, *adv.* word unexplained and not yet satisfactorily amended. L.L.L. V. 2. 67.

Pervert, *v.t.* to avert, turn aside.

Pettitoes, *sb.* feet; properly pig's feet.

Pheeze, *v.t.* beat, chastise, torment.

Phisnomy, *sb.* physiognomy.

Phraseless, *adj.* indescribable.

Physical, *adj.* salutary, wholesome.

Pia mater, *sb.* membrane that covers the brain; used for the brain itself.

Pick, *v.t.* to pitch, throw.

Picked, *p.p.* refined, precise.

Picking, *adj.* trifling, small.

Piece, *sb.* a vessel of wine.

Pight, *p.p.* pitched.

Piled, *p.p* = peeled, bald, with quibble on 'piled' of velvet.

Pill, *v.t.* to pillage, plunder.

Pin, *sb.* bull's-eye of a target.

Pin-buttock, *sb.* a narrow buttock.

Pioned, *adj.* doubtful word: perhaps covered with marsh-marigold, or simply dug.

Pip, *sb.* a spot on cards. A pip out = intoxicated, with reference to a game called one and thirty.

Pitch, *sb.* the height to which a falcon soars, height.

Placket, *sb.* opening in a petticoat, or a petticoat.

Planched, *adj.* made of planks.

Plantage, *sb.* plants, vegetation.

Plantation, *sb.* colonizing.

Plausive, *adj.* persuasive, pleasing.

Pleached, *adj.* interlaced, folded.

Plurisy, *sb.* superabundance.

Point-devise, *adj.* precise, finical. L.L.L. V. 1.19. *adv.* Tw.N. II. 5. 162.

Poking-sticks, *sb.* irons for setting out ruffs.

Pole-clipt, *adj.* used of vineyards in which the vines are grown around poles.

Polled, *adj.* clipped, laid bare.

Pomander, *sb.* a ball of perfume.

Poor-John, *sb.* salted and dried hake.

Porpentine, *sb.* porcupine.

Portable, *adj.* supportable, endurable.

Portage, *sb.* port-hole. H V. III. 1. 10. Port-dues. Per. III. 1. 35.

Portance, *sb.* deportment, bearing.

Posse, *v.t.* to curdle.

Posy, *sb.* a motto on a ring.

Potch, *v.i.* to poke, thrust.

Pottle, *sb.* a tankard; strictly a two quart measure.

Pouncet-box, *sb.* a box for perfumes, pierced with holes.

Practice, *sb.* plot.

Practisant, *sb.* accomplice.

Practise, *v.i.* to plot, use stratagems. Two G. IV. 1. 47. *v.t.* to plot. John, IV. 1. 20.

Precedent, *sb.* rough draft. R III. III. 6. 7. Prognostic, indication. V. & A. 26.

Prefer, *v.t.* to promote, advance. Two G. II. 4. 154. Recommend. Cym. II. 3. 50. Present offer. M.N.D. IV. 2. 37.

Pregnant, *adj.* ready-witted, clever. Tw.N. II. 2. 28. Full of meaning. Ham. II. 2. 209. Ready. Ham. III. 2. 66. Plain, evident. M. for M. II. I. 23.

Prenzie, *adj.* demure.

Pretence, *sb.* project, scheme.

Prick, *sb.* point on a dial. 3 H VI. I. 4. 34. Bull's-eye. L.L.L. IV. I. 132. Prickle. As III. 2. 113. Skewer. Lear, II. 3. 16.

Pricket, *sb.* a buck of the second year.

Prick-song, *sb.* music sung from notes.

Prig, *sb.* a thief.

Private, *sb.* privacy. Tw.N. III. 4. 90. Private communication. John, IV. 3. 16.

Prize, *sb.* prize-contest. T.A. I. I. 399. Privilege. 3 H VI. I. 4. 59. Value. Cym. III. 6. 76.

Probal, *adj.* probable, reasonable.

Proditor, *sb.* traitor.

Proface, *int.* much good may it do you!

Propagate, *v.t.* to augment.

Propagation, *sb.* augmentation.

Proper-false, *adj.* handsome and deceitful.

Property, *sb.* a tool or instrument. M.W.W. III. 4. 10. *v.t.* to make a tool of. John, V. 2. 79.

Pugging, *adj.* thievish.

Puisny, *adj.* unskilful, like a tyro.

Pun, *v.t.* to pound.

Punk, *sb.* strumpet.

Purchase, *v.t.* to acquire, get. *sb.* acquisition, booty.

Pursuivant, *sb.* a herald's attendant or messenger.

Pursy, *adj.* short-winded, asthmatic.

Puttock, *sb.* a kite.

Puzzel, *sb.* a filthy drab (Italian *puzzolente*).

Quaintly, *adv.* ingeniously, deliberately.

Qualification, *sb.* appeasement.

Quality, *sb.* profession, calling, especially that of an actor. Two G. IV. 1. 58. Professional skill. Tp. I. 2. 193.

Quarter, *sb.* station. John, V. 5. 20. Keep fair quarter = keep on good terms with, be true to. C. of E. II. 1. 108. In quarter = on good terms. Oth. II. 3. 176.

Quat, *sb.* pimple.

Quatch-buttock, *sb.* a squat or flat buttock.

Quean, *sb.* wench, hussy.

Queasiness, *sb.* nausea, disgust.

Queasy, *adj.* squeamish, fastidious. M.A. II. 1. 368. Disgusted. A. & C. III. 6. 20.

Quell, *sb.* murder.

Quest, *sb.* inquest, jury. R III. I. 4. 177. Search, inquiry, pursuit. M. of V. I. 1. 172. A body of searchers. Oth. I. 2. 46.

Questant, *sb.* aspirant, candidate.

Quicken, *v.t.* to make alive. A.W. II. 1. 76. Refresh, revive. M. of V. II. 7. 52. *v.i.* to become alive, revive. Lear, III. 7. 40.

Quietus, *sb.* settlement of an account.

Quill, *sb.* body. 2 H VI. I. 3. 3.

Quillet, *sb.* quibble.

Quintain, *sb.* a figure set up for tilting at.

Quire, *sb.* company.

Quittance, *v.i.* to requite. 1 H VI. II. 1. 14. *sb.* acquittance. M. W. W. I. 1. 10. Requital. 2 H IV. I. 1. 108.

Quoif, *sb.* cap.

Quoit, *v.t.* to throw.

Quote, *v.t.* to note, examine.

Rabato, *sb.* a kind of ruff.

Rabbit-sucker, *sb.* sucking rabbit.

Race, *sb.* root. W.T. IV. 3. 48. Nature, disposition. M. for M. II. 4. 160. Breed. Mac. II. 4. 15.

Rack, *v.t.* stretch, strain. M. of V. I. 1. 181. Strain to the utmost. Cor. V. 1. 16.

Rack, *sb.* a cloud or mass of clouds. Ham. II. 2. 492. *v.i.* move like vapour. 3 H VI. II. 1. 27.

Rampired, *p.p.* fortified by a rampart.

Ramps, *sb.* wanton wenches.

Ranges, *sb.* ranks.

Rap, *v.t.* to transport.

Rascal, *sb.* a deer out of condition.

Raught, *impf.* & *p.p.* reached.

Rayed, *p.p.* befouled. T. of S. IV. 1. 3. In T. of S. III. 2. 52 it perhaps means arrayed, *i.e.* attacked.

Raze, *sb.* root.

Razed, *p.p.* slashed.

Reave, *v.t.* to bereave.

Rebate, *v.t.* to make dull, blunt.

Recheat, *sb.* a set of notes sounded to call hounds off a false scent.

Rede, *sb.* counsel.

Reechy, *adj.* smoky, grimy.

Refell, *v.t.* to refute.

Refuse, *sb.* rejection, disowning. *v.t.* to reject, disown.

Reguerdon, *v.t.* to reward, guerdon.

Remonstrance, *sb.* demonstration.

Remotion, *sb.* removal.

Renege, *v.t.* to deny.

Renying, *pres. p.* denying.

Replication, *sb.* echo. J.C. I. 1. 50. Reply. Ham. IV. 2. 12.

Rere-mice, *sb.* bats.

Respected, blunder for suspected.

Respective, *adj.* worthy of regard. Two G. IV. 4. 197. Showing regard. John, I. 1. 188. Careful. M. of V. V. 1. 156.

Respectively, *adv.* respectfully.

Rest, *sb.* set up one's rest is to stand upon the cards in one's hand, be fully resolved.

Resty, *adj.* idle, lazy.

Resume, *v.t.* to take.

Reverb, *v.t.* to resound.

Revolt, *sb.* rebel.

Ribaudred, *adj.* ribald, lewd.

Rid, *v.t.* to destroy, do away with.

Riggish, *adj.* wanton.

Rigol, *sb.* a circle.

Rim, *sb.* midriff or abdomen.

Rivage, *sb.* shore.

Rival, *sb.* partner, companion. M.N.D. III. 2. 156. *v.i.* to be a competitor. Lear, I. 1. 191.

Rivality, *sb.* partnership, participation.

Rivelled, *adj.* wrinkled.

Road, *sb.* roadstead, port. Two G. II. 4. 185. Journey. H VIII. IV. 2. 17. Inroad, incursion. H V. I. 2. 138.

Roisting, *adj.* roistering, blustering.

Romage, *sb.* bustle, turmoil.

Ronyon, *sb.* scurvy wretch.

Rook, *v.i.* to cower, squat.

Ropery, *sb.* roguery.

Rope-tricks, *sb.* knavish tricks.

Roping, *pr.p.* dripping.

Roted, *p.p.* learned by heart.

Rother, *sb.* an ox, or animal of the ox kind.

Round, *v.i.* to whisper. John, II. 1. 566. *v.t.* to surround. M.N.D. IV. 1. 52.

Round, *adj.* straightforward, blunt, plainspoken. C. of E. II. 1. 82.

Rouse, *sb.* deep draught, bumper.

Rout, *sb.* crowd, mob. C. of E. III. 1. 101. Brawl. Oth. II. 3. 210.

Row, *sb.* verse or stanza.

Roynish, *adj.* scurvy; hence coarse, rough.

Rub, *v.i.* to encounter obstacles. L.L.L. IV. 1. 139. Rub on, of a bowl that surmounts the obstacle in its course. T. & C. III. 2. 49. *sb.* impediment, hindrance; from the game of bowls. John, III. 4. 128.

Ruffle, *v.i.* to swagger, bully. T.A. I. 1. 314.

Ruddock, *sb.* the redbreast.

Rudesby, *sb.* a rude fellow.

Rump-fed, *adj.* pampered; perhaps fed on offal, or else fat-rumped.

Running banquet, a hasty refreshment (fig.).

Rush aside, *v.t.* to pass hastily by, thrust aside.

Rushling, blunder for rustling.

Sad, *adj.* grave, serious. M. of V. II. 2. 195. Gloomy, sullen. R II. V. 5. 70.

Sagittary, *sb.* a centaur. T. & C. V. 5. 14. The official residence in the arsenal at Venice. Oth. I. 1. 160.

Sallet, *sb.* a close-fitting helmet. 2 H VI. IV. 10. 11. A salad. 2 H VI. IV. 10. 8.

Salt, *sb.* salt-cellar. Two G. III. 1. 354. *adj.* lecherous. M. for M. V. 1. 399. Stinging, bitter. T. & C. I. 3. 371.

Salutation, *sb.* give salutation to my blood = make my blood rise.

Salute, *v.t.* to meet. John, II. 1. 590. To affect. H VIII. II. 3. 103.

Sanded, *adj.* sandy-coloured.

Say, *sb.* a kind of silk.

Scald, *adj.* scurvy, scabby. H V. V. 1. 5.

Scale, *v.t.* to put in the scales, weigh.

Scall = scald. M.W.W. III. 1. 115.

Scamble, *v.i.* to scramble.

Scamel, *sb.* perhaps a misprint for seamell, or seamew.

Scantling, *sb.* a scanted or small portion.

Scape, *sb.* freak, escapade.

Sconce, *sb.* a round fort. H V. III. 6. 73. Hence a protection for the head. C. of E. II. 2. 37. Hence the skull. Ham. V. 1. 106. *v.r.* to ensconce, hide. Ham. III. 4. 4.

Scotch, *sb.* notch. *v.t.* to cut, slash.

Scrowl, *v.i.* perhaps for to scrawl.

Scroyles, *sb.* scabs, scrofulous wretches.

Scrubbed, *adj.* undersized.

Scull, *sb.* shoal of fish.

Seal, *sb.* to give seals = confirm, carry out.

Seam, *sb.* grease, lard.

Seconds, *sb.* an inferior kind of flour.

Secure, *adj.* without care, confident.

Security, *sb.* carelessness, want of caution.

Seedness, *sb.* sowing with seed.

Seel, *v.t.* to close up a hawk's eyes.

Self-admission, *sb.* self-approbation.

Semblative, *adj.* resembling, like.

Sequestration, *sb.* separation.

Serpigo, *sb.* tetter or eruption on the skin.

Sessa, *int.* exclamation urging to speed.

Shard-borne, *adj.* borne through the air on shards.

Shards, *sb.* the wing cases of beetles. A. & C. III. 2. 20. Potsherds. Ham. V. I. 254.

Sharked up, *p.p.* gathered indiscriminately.

Shealed, *p.p.* shelled.

Sheep-biter, *sb.* a malicious, niggardly fellow.

Shent, *p.p.* scolded, rebuked. M.W.W. I. 4. 36.

Shive, *sb.* slice.

Shog, *v.i.* to move, jog.

Shore, *sb.* a sewer.

Shrewd, *adj.* mischievous, bad.

Shrewdly, *adv.* badly.

Shrewdness, *sb.* mischievousness.

Shrieve, *sb.* sheriff.

Shrowd, *sb.* shelter, protection.

Siege, *sb.* seat. M. for M. IV. 2. 98. Rank. Ham. IV. 7. 75. Excrement. Tp. II. 2. 111.

Significant, *sb.* sign, token.

Silly, *adj.* harmless, innocent. Two G. IV. 1. 72. Plain, simple. Tw.N. II. 4. 46.

Simular, *adj.* simulated, counterfeited. Cym. V. 5. 20. *sb.* simulator, pretender. Lear, III. 2. 54.

Sitch, *adv.* and *conj.* since.

Skains-mates, *sb.* knavish companions.

Slab, *adj.* slabby, slimy.

Sleeve-hand, *sb.* wristband.

Sleided, *adj.* untwisted.

Slipper, *adj.* slippery.

Slobbery, *adj.* dirty.

Slubber, *v.t.* to slur over, do carelessly.

Smatch, *sb.* smack, taste.

Sneak-cup, *sb.* a fellow who shirks his liquor.

Sneap, *v.t.* to pinch, nip. L.L.L. I. 1. 100. *sb.* snub, reprimand. 2 H IV. II. 1. 125.

Sneck up, contemptuous expression = go and be hanged.

Snuff, *sb.* quarrel. Lear, III. 1. 26. Smouldering wick of a candle. Cym. I. 6. 87. Object of contempt. A.W. I. 2. 60. Take in snuff = take offence at. L.L.L. V. 2. 22.

Sob, *sb.* a rest given to a horse to regain its wind.

Solidare, *sb.* a small coin.

Sonties, *sb.* corruption of saints.

Sooth, *sb.* flattery.

Soothers, *sb.* flatterers.

Sophy, *sb.* the Shah of Persia.

Sore, *sb.* a buck of the fourth year.

Sorel, *sb.* a buck of the third year.

Sort, *sb.* rank. M.A. I. 1. 6. Set, company. R III. V. 3. 316. Manner. M. of V. I. 2. 105. Lot. T. & C. I. 3. 376.

Sort, *v.t.* to pick out. Two G. III. 2. 92. To rank. Ham. II. 2. 270. To arrange, dispose. R III. II. 2. 148. To adapt. 2 H VI. II. 4. 68. *v.i.* to associate. V. & A. 689. To be fitting. T. & C. I. 1. 109. Fall out, happen. M.N.D. III. 2. 352.

Souse, *v.t.* to swoop down on, as a falcon.

Sowl, *v.t.* to lug, drag by the ears.

Span-counter, *sb.* boy's game of throwing a counter so as to strike, or rest within a span of, an opponent's counter.

Speed, *sb.* fortune, success.

Speken = speak.

Sperr, *v.t.* to bar.

Spital, *sb.* hospital.

Spital house, *sb.* hospital.

Spleen, *sb.* quick movement. M.N.D. I. 1. 146. Fit of laughter. L.L.L. III. 1. 76.

Spot, *sb.* pattern in embroidery.

Sprag, *adj.* sprack, quick, lively.

Spring, *sb.* a young shoot.

Springhalt, *sb.* a lameness in horses.

Spurs, *sb.* the side roots of a tree.

Squandering, *adj.* roving, random. As II. 7. 57.

Square, *sb.* the embroidery about the bosom of a smock or shift. W.T. IV. 3. 212. Most precious square of sense = the most sensitive part. Lear, I. 1. 74.

Square, *v.i.* to quarrel.

Squash, *sb.* an unripe peascod.

Squier, *sb.* square, rule.

Squiny, *v.i.* to look asquint.

Staggers, *sb.* giddiness, bewilderment. A.W. II. 3. 164. A disease of horses. T. of S. III. 2. 53.

Stale, *sb.* laughing stock, dupe. 3 H VI. III. 3. 260. Decoy. T. of S. III. 1. 90. Stalking-horse. C. of E. II. 1. 101. Prostitute. M.A. II. 2. 24. Horse-urine. A. & C. I. 4. 62.

Stamp, *v.t.* to mark as genuine, give currency to.

Standing, *sb.* duration, continuance. W.T. I. 2. 430. Attitude. Tim. I. 1. 34.

Standing-tuck, *sb.* a rapier standing on end.

Staniel, *sb.* a hawk, the kestrel.

Stare, *v.i.* to stand on end.

State, *sb.* attitude. L.L.L. IV. 3. 183. A chair of state. 1 H IV. II. 4. 390. Estate, fortune. M. of V. III. 2. 258. States (pl.) = persons of high position. John, II. 1. 395.

Statute-caps, *sb.* woollen caps worn by citizens as decreed by the Act of 1571.

Staves, *sb.* shafts of lances.

Stead, *v.t.* to help.

Stead up, *v.t.* to take the place of.

Stelled, *p.p.* fixed. Lucr. 1444. Sonn. XXIV. 1. Starry. Lear, III. 7. 62.

Stickler-like, *adj.* like a stickler, whose duty it was to separate combatants.

Stigmatic, *adj.* marked by deformity.

Stillitory, *sb.* a still.

Stint, *v.i.* to stop, cease. R. & J. I. 3. 48. *v.t.* to check, stop. T. & C. IV. 5. 93.

Stock, *sb.* a dowry. Two G. III. 1. 305. A stocking. Two G. III. 1. 306; 1 H IV. II. 4. 118. A thrust in fencing. M.W.W. II. 3. 24. *v.t.* to put in the stocks. Lear, II. 2. 333.

Stomach, *sb.* courage. 2 H IV. I. 1. 129. Pride. T. of S. V. 2. 177.

Stomaching, *sb.* resentment.

Stone-bow, *sb.* a cross-bow for shooting stones.

Stoop, *sb.* a drinking vessel.

Stricture, *sb.* strictness.

Stride, *v.t.* to overstep.

Stover, *sb.* cattle fodder.

Stuck, *sb.* a thrust in fencing.

Subject, *sb.* subjects, collectively.

Subscribe, *v.i.* to be surety. A.W. III. 6. 84. Yield, submit. 1 H VI. II. 4. 44. *v.t.* to admit, acknowledge. M.A. V. 2. 58.

Subtle, *adj.* deceptively smooth.

Successantly, *adv.* in succession.

Sufferance, *sb.* suffering. M. for M. II. 2. 167. Patience. M. of V. I. 3. 109. Loss. Oth. II. 1. 23. Death penalty. H V. II. 2. 158.

Suggest, *v.t.* to tempt.

Suit, *sb.* service, attendance. M. for M. IV. 4. 19. Out of suits with fortune = out of fortune's service.

Supervise, *sb.* inspection.

Suppliance, *sb.* pastime.

Sur-addition, *sb.* an added title.

Surmount, *v.i.* to surpass, exceed. 1 H VI. V. 3. 191. *v.t.* to surpass. L.L.L. V. 2. 677.

Sur-reined, *p.p.* overridden.

Suspect, *sb.* suspicion.

Swarth, *adj.* black. T.A. II. 3. 71. *sb.* swath. Tw.N. II. 3. 145.

Swoopstake, *adv.* in one sweep, wholesale.

Tag, *sb.* rabble.

Take, *v.t.* to captivate. W.T. IV. 3. 119. Strike. M.W.W. IV. 4. 32. Take refuge in. C. of E. V. 1. 36. Leap over. John,

V. 2. 138. Take in = conquer. A. & C. I. 1.23. Take out = copy. Oth. III. 3. 296. Take thought = feel grief for. J.C. II. 1. 187. Take up = get on credit. 2 H VI. IV. 7. 125. Reconcile. Tw.N. III. 4. 294. Rebuke. Two G. I. 2. 134.

Tallow-keech, *sb.* a vessel filled with tallow.

Tanling, *sb.* one tanned by the sun. John, IV. 1. 117. Incite. Ham. II. 2. 358.

Tarre, *v.t.* to set on dogs to fight.

Taste, *sb.* trial, proof. *v.t.* to try, prove.

Tawdry-lace, *sb.* a rustic necklace.

Taxation, *sb.* satire, censure. As I. 2. 82. Claim, demand. Tw.N. I. 5. 210.

Teen, *sb.* grief.

Tenable, *adj.* capable of being kept.

Tend, *v.i.* to wait, attend. Ham. I. 3. 83. Be attentive. Tp. I. 1. 6. *v.t.* to tend to, regard. 2 H VI. I. 1. 204. Wait upon. A. & C. II. 2. 212.

Tendance, *sb.* attention. Tim. I. 1. 60. Persons attending. Tim. I. 1. 74.

Tender, *v.t.* to hold dear, regard. R III. I. 1. 44. *sb.* care, regard. 1 H IV. V. 4. 49.

Tender-hefted, *adj.* set in a delicate handle or frame.

Tent, *sb.* probe. T. & C. II. 2. 16. *v.t.* to probe. Ham. II. 2. 608. Cure. Cor. I. 9. 31.

Tercel, *sb.* male goshawk.

Termless, *adj.* not to be described.

Testerned, *p.p.* presented with sixpence.

Testril, *sb.* sixpence.

Tetchy, *adj.* irritable.

Tetter, *sb.* skin erruption. Ham. I. 5. 71. *v.t.* to infect with tetter. Cor. III. 1. 99.

Than = then, Lucr. 1440.

Tharborough, *sb.* third borough, constable.

Thick, *adv.* rapidly, close.

Thirdborough, *sb.* constable.

Thisne, perhaps = in this way. M.N.D. I. 2. 48.

Thoughten, *p.p.* be you thoughten = entertain the thought.

Thrall, *sb.* thraldom, slavery. Pass. P. 266. *adj.* enslaved. V. & A. 837.

Three-man beetle, a rammer operated by three men.

Three-man songmen, three-part glee-singers.

Three-pile, *sb.* the finest kind of velvet.

Three-piled, *adj.* having a thick pile. M. for M. I. 2. 32. Superfine (met.). L.L.L. V. 2. 407.

Tickle, *adj.* unstable. 2 H VI. I. I. 216. Tickle of the sere, used of lungs readily prompted to laughter; literally hair-triggered. Ham. II. 2. 329.

Ticklish, *adj.* wanton.

Tight, *adj.* swift, deft. A. & C. IV. 4. 15. Water-tight, sound. T. of S. II. I. 372.

Tightly, *adv.* briskly, smartly.

Time-pleaser, *sb.* time server, one who complies with the times.

Tire, *sb.* headdress. Two G. IV. 4. 187. Furniture. Per II. 2. 21.

Tire, *v.i.* to feed greedily. 3 H VI. I. I. 269. *v.t.* make to feed greedily. Lucr. 417.

Tisick, *sb.* phthisic, a cough.

Toaze, *v.t.* to draw out, untangle.

Tod, *sb.* Twenty-eight pounds of wool. *v.t.* to yield a tod.

Toged, *adj.* wearing a toga.

Toll, *v.i.* to pay toll. A.W. V. 3. 147. *v.t.* to take toll. John, III. I. 154.

Touch, *sb.* trait. As V. 4. 27. Dash, spice. R III. IV. 4. 157. Touchstone. R III. IV. 2. 8. Of noble touch = of tried nobility. Cor. IV. I. 49. Brave touch = fine test of valour. M.N.D. III. 2. 70. Slight hint. H VIII. V. I. 13. Know no touch = have no skill. R II. I. 3. 165.

Touse, *v.t.* to pull, tear.

Toy, *sb.* trifle, idle fancy, folly.

Tract, *sb.* track, trace. Tim. I. I. 53. Course. H VIII. I. I. 40.

Train, *v.t.* to allure, decoy. 1 H VI. I. 3. 25. *sb.* bait, allurement. Mac. IV. 3. 118.

Tranect, *sb.* ferry, a doubtful word.

Translate, *v.t.* to transform.

Trash, *v.t.* lop off branches. Tp. I. 2. 81. Restrain a dog by a trash or strap. Oth. II. 1. 307.

Traverse, *v.i.* to march to the right or left.

Tray-trip, *sb.* a game at dice, which was won by throwing a trey.

Treachors, *sb.* traitors.

Treatise, *sb.* discourse.

Trench, *v.t.* to cut. Two G. III. 2. 7. Divert from its course by digging. H IV. III. 1. 112.

Troll-my-dames, *sb.* the French game of *trou madame*, perhaps akin to bagatelle.

Tropically, *adv.* figuratively.

True-penny, *sb.* an honest fellow. Ham. I. 5. 150.

Try, *sb.* trial, test. Tim. VI. 1. 9. Bring to try = bring a ship as close to the wind as possible.

Tub, *sb.* and tubfast, *sb.* a cure of venereal disease by sweating and fasting.

Tuck, *sb.* rapier.

Tun-dish, *sb.* funnel.

Turk, to turn Turk = to be a renegade. M.A. III. 4. 52. Turk Gregory = Pope Gregory VII. I H IV. V. 3. 125.

Twiggen, *adj.* made of twigs or wicker.

Twilled, *adj.* perhaps, covered with sedge or reeds.

Twire, *v.i.* to twinkle.

Umber, *sb.* a brown colour.

Umbered, *p.p.* made brown, darkened.

Umbrage, *sb.* a shadow.

Unaneled, *adj.* not having received extreme unction.

Unbarbed, *adj.* wearing no armour, bare.

Unbated, *adj.* unblunted.

Unbraced, *adj.* unbuttoned.

Uncape, *v.i.* to uncouple, throw off the hounds.

Uncase, *v.i.* to undress.

Unclew, *v.t.* to unwind, undo.

Uncolted, *p.p.* deprived of one's horse. I H IV. II. 2. 41.

Uncomprehensive, *adj.* incomprehensible.

Unconfirmed, *adj.* inexperienced.

Undercrest, *v.t.* to wear upon the crest.

Undertaker, *sb.* agent, person responsible to another for something.

Underwrite, *v.t.* to submit to.

Undistinguished, *adj.* not to be seen distinctly, unknowable.

Uneath, *adv.* hardly, with difficulty.

Unfolding, *adj.* unfolding star, the star at whose rising the shepherd lets the sheep out of the fold.

Unhappy, *adj.* mischievous, unlucky.

Unhatched, *p.p.* unhacked. Tw.N. III. 4. 234. Undisclosed. Oth. III. 4. 140.

Unhouseled, *adj.* without having received the sacrament.

Union, *sb.* large pearl.

Unkind, *adj.* unnatural. Lear, I. I. 261. Childless. V. & A. 204.

Unlived, *p.p.* deprived of life.

Unpaved, *adj.* without stones.

Unpinked, *adj.* not pinked, or pierced with eyelet holes.

Unraked, *adj.* not made up for the night.

Unrecuring, *adj.* incurable.

Unrolled, *p.p.* struck off the roll.

Unseeming, *pr.p.* not seeming.

Unseminared, *p.p.* deprived of seed or virility.

Unset, *adj.* unplanted.

Unshunned, *adj.* inevitable.

Unsifted, *adj.* untried, inexperienced.

Unsquared, *adj.* unsuitable.

Unstate, *v.t.* to deprive of dignity.

Untented, *adj.* incurable.

Unthrift, *sb.* prodigal. *adj.* good for nothing.

Untraded, *adj.* unhackneyed.

Unyoke, *v.t.* to put off the yoke, take ease after labour. Ham. V. I. 55. *v.t.* to disjoin. John, III. I. 241.

Up-cast, *sb.* a throw at bowls; perhaps the final throw.

Upshoot, *sb.* decisive shot.

Upspring, *sb.* a bacchanalian dance.

Upstaring, *adj.* standing on end.

Urchin, *sb.* hedgehog. T.A. II. 3. 101. A goblin. M.W.W. IV. 4. 49.

Usance, *sb.* interest.

Use, *sb.* interest. M.A. II. 1. 269. Usage. M. for M. I. 1. 40. In use = in trust. M. of V. IV. 1. 383.

Use, *v.r.* to behave oneself.

Uses, *sb.* manners, usages.

Utis, *sb.* boisterous merriment.

Vade, *v.i.* to fade.

Vail, *sb.* setting (of the sun). T. & C. V. 8. 7. *v.t.* to lower, let fall. 1 H VI. V. 3. 25. *v.i.* to bow. Per. IV. Prol. 29.

Vails, *sb.* a servant's perquisites.

Vain, for vain = to no purpose.

Vantbrace, *sb.* armour for the forearm.

Vast, *adj.* waste, desolate, boundless.

Vaunt-couriers, *sb.* fore-runners.

Vaward, *sb.* vanguard. 1 H VI. I. 1. 132. The first part. M.N.D. IV. 1. 106.

Vegetives, *sb.* plants.

Velvet-guards, *sb.* velvet linings, used metaphorically of those who wear them. 1 H IV. III. 1. 256.

Veney, or venew, *sb.* a fencing bout, a hit.

Venge, *v.t.* to avenge.

Vent, *sb.* discharge. Full of vent = effervescent like wine.

Via, *interj.* away, on!

Vice, *sb.* the buffoon in old morality plays. R III. III. 1. 82. *v.t.* to screw (met.) W.T. I. 2. 415.

Vinewedst, *adj.* mouldy, musty.

Violent, *v.i.* to act violently, rage.

Virginalling, *pr.p.* playing with the fingers as upon the virginals.

Virtuous, *adj.* efficacious, powerful. Oth. III. 4 .110. Essential. M.N.D. III. 2. 367. Virtuous season = benignant influence. M. for M. II. 2. 168.

Vouch, *sb.* testimony, guarantee. 1 H VI. V. 3. 71. *v.i.* to assert, warrant.

Vizard, *sb.* mask.

Waft, *v.t.* to beckon. C. of E. II. 2. 108. To turn. W.T. I. 2. 371.

Wag, *v.i.* and *v.t.* to move, stir. R III. III. 5. 7. To go one's way. M.A. V. 1. 16.

Wage, *v.t.* to stake, risk. 1 H IV. 4. 20. *v.i.* to contend. Lear, II. 4. 210. Wage equal = be on an equality with. A. & C. v. 1. 31.

Wanion, *sb.* with a wanion = with a vengeance.

Wanton, *sb.* one brought up in luxury, an effeminate person. John, V. 1. 70. *v.i.* to dally, play. W.T. II. 1. 18.

Wappened, *p.p.* of doubtful meaning, perhaps worn out, stale.

Ward, *sb.* guardianship. A.W. I. 1. 5. Defence. L.L.L. III. 1. 131. Guard in fencing. 1 H IV. II. 4. 198. Prison, custody. 2 H VI. V. 1. 112. Lock, bolt. Tim. III. 3. 38. *v.t.* to guard. R III. V. 3. 254.

Warden-pies, *sb.* pies made with the warden, a large baking pear.

Warrantize, *sb.* security, warranty.

Warrener, *sb.* keeper of a warren, gamekeeper.

Watch, *sb.* a watch candle that marked the hours.

Watch, *v.t.* to tame by keeping from sleep.

Waters, *sb.* for all waters = ready for anything.

Wealsmen, *sb.* statesmen.

Web and pin. *sb.* cataract of the eye.

Weeding, *sb.* weeds.

Weet, *v.t.* to know.

Welkin, *sb.* the blue, the sky. Tw.N. II. 3. 61. *adj.* sky-blue. W.T. I. 2. 136.

Whiffler, *sb.* one who cleared the way for a procession, carrying the whiffle or staff of his office.

Whist, *adj.* still, hushed.

Whittle, *sb.* a clasp-knife.

Whoobub, *sb*. hubbub.

Widowhood, *sb*. rights as a widow.

Wilderness, *sb*. wildness.

Wimpled, *p.p*. blindfolded. (A wimple was a wrap or handkerchief for the neck.)

Winchester goose, *sb*. a venereal swelling in the groin, the brothels of Southwark being in the jurisdiction of the Bishop of Winchester.

Window-bars, *sb*. lattice-like embroidery worn by women across the breast.

Windring, *adj*. winding.

Wink, *sb*. a closing of the eyes, sleep. Tp. II. 1. 281. *v.i*. to close the eyes, be blind, be in the dark. C. of E. III. 2. 58.

Winter-ground, *v.t*. to protect a plant from frost by bedding it with straw.

Wipe, *sb*. a brand, mark of shame.

Wise-woman, *sb*. a witch.

Witch, *sb*. used of a man also; wizard.

Woman, *v.t*. woman me = make me show my woman's feelings.

Woman-tired, *adj*. henpecked.

Wondered, *p.p*. performing wonders.

Wood, *adj*. mad.

Woodman, *sb*. forester, hunter. M.W.W. V. 5. 27. In a bad sense, a wencher. M. for M. IV. 4. 163.

Woollen, to lie in the = either to lie in the blankets, or to be buried in flannel, as the law in Shakespeare's time prescribed.

Word, *sb*. to be at a word = to be as good as one's word.

Word, *v.t*. to represent. Cym. I. 4. 15. To deceive with words. A. & C. V. 2. 191.

World, *sb*. to go to the world = to be married. A woman of the world = a married woman. A world to see = a marvel to behold.

Wrangler, *sb*. an opponent, a tennis term.

Wreak, *sb*. revenge. T.A. IV. 3. 33. *v.t*. to revenge. T.A. IV. 3. 51.

Wreakful, *adj.* revengeful.

Wrest, *sb.* a tuning-key.

Wring, *v.i.* to writhe.

Write, *v.r.* to describe oneself, claim to be. Writ as little beard = claimed as little beard. A.W. II. 3. 62.

Writhled, *adj.* shrivelled up, wrinkled.

Wry, *v.i.* to swerve.

Yare, *adj.* and *adv.* ready, active, nimble.

Yarely, *adv.* readily, briskly.

Yearn, *v.t.* and *v.i.* to grieve.

Yellows, *sb.* jaundice in horses.

Yerk, *v.t.* to lash out at, strike quickly.

Yest, *sb.* froth, foam.

Yesty, *adj.* foamy, frothy.

Younker, *sb.* a stripling, youngster novice.

Yslaked, *p.p.* brought to rest.

Zany, *sb.* a fool, buffoon.

BIBLIOGRAPHY

Ackroyd, Peter, *Shakespeare: The Biography*, Vintage, 2006

Bloom, Harold, *William Shakespeare's Henry V: Modern Critical Interpretations*, Chelsea House, 1988

Foakes, R.A., *Shakespeare and Violence*, Cambridge University Press, 2003

Halliday, F.E., *A Shakespeare Companion*, Penguin, 1964

Holden, Anthony, *William Shakespeare: An Illustrated Biography*, Little, Brown, 2002

Jarman, Rosemary Hawley, *Crispin's Day: The Glory of Agincourt*, Little, Brown, 1979

Langston, David, *York Notes on Shakespeare's Henry V*, Longman, 1998

Quinn, Michael, *Shakespeare: Henry V: A Casebook*, Macmillan, 1969

Watts, Cedric, *Henry V War Criminal? And Other Shakespeare Puzzles*, OUP, 2000